D0900763

STUCK IN THE GAME

Praise for The Dream State Saga

"The only thing I didn't love about this series was that I didn't write it!"
—G. R. Cooper, author of the *Omegaverse* series

"Fans of LitRPG and video games need to be reading Christopher Keene."
—Paul Mannering, President of SpecFicNZ, author of *Engines of Empathy*

"Dream State has great usage of hyperrealism and surrealism that draws you deeply into the story. With excellent grammar and smooth dialogue, it's hard to put the book down!"
—Dakota Krout, author of *The Divine Dungeon* series

Books and Series featuring Christopher Keene

A Beginner's Guide to Summoning
a short story

War of Kings and Monsters

Super Dungeon Series

The King's Summons
Adam Glendon Sidwell and Zachary James

The Forgotten King
D. W. Vogel

The Glauerdoom Moor
David J. West

The Dungeons of Arcadia
Dan Allen

The Midnight Queen
Christopher Keene

DREAM STATE SAGA

Stuck in the Game
First in the Game
a short story

Dedicated to Aidan Smith. This book is a result of our numerous discussions.

Stuck in the Game

Future House Publishing

Cover image copyright: Shutterstock.com. Used under license.

Text © 2021 Christopher Keene

All rights reserved. No part of this book may be reproduced in any form or by any means without the written permission of Future House Publishing at rights@futurehousepublishing.com.
This book is a work of fiction. Names, characters, places, and incidents are either the product of the author's imagination or are used fictitiously. Any resemblance to actual persons, living or dead, or to actual events or locales is entirely coincidental.

ISBN: 978-1-950020-52-2

Developmental editing by Mandi Diaz and Emma Heggem
Substantive editing by Emma Heggem
Copy editing by Alexa McKaig and Kennadie Halliday
Proofreading by Dara Johnson and Sheridan Bird
Interior design by Madeline Jones

STUCK IN THE GAME

CHRISTOPHER KEENE

Future House Publishing

Chapter 1
DREAM ENGINE

I didn't know how long I had been floating in the darkness. My body twitched as waves of anxiety and exhilaration crashed over me, drowning me.

When the tides of emotion finally receded, my heartbeat calmed, and I floated once more, trying to gain a sense of my surroundings.

A speck of light appeared before me, glowing like the first glimpse of a sunrise after a starless night. The white radiance grew until the circle was as wide as I was tall. As bright as the light was, my eyes seemed to have already adjusted to it.

Three smaller lights appeared around the circle, forming words I couldn't quite make out until I gave them my full attention. Of the three lights, "New Game" glowed the brightest. The other two read "Continue" and "Settings." I had played enough video games to recognize a gaming menu when I saw one.

"New Game?" The sound of my voice was jarring after the silence.

The icon flashed and the words were sucked into the circle of light, like being drawn into a whirlpool. I followed them soon after, my body stretching as the light engulfed me, and a brief whine filled my ears.

When the light faded, I was standing on a dirt pathway surrounded by the greenest field of grass I had ever seen, complete with daisies and dandelions. I expected to smell the grass, but when I sniffed the air, I couldn't identify a single distinguishable scent. My sniff seemed to be the loudest noise around. Everything from the clouds in the azure sky to the distant trees had the look of a CGI wallpaper. Every object had been so neatly arranged that it only highlighted how unnatural it all was.

It isn't real. My eyebrows knitted together in confusion.

I touched the dirt of the pathway, feeling its rough texture under my fingertips. It felt too real, if such a sensation was possible. The edges of the track were cleanly cut, despite the high grass surrounding it. I saw a split in the path in the distance, and ahead of me, on the side of the pathway, was a wooden sign pegged into the grass. I walked forward, blurry details of the environment far away becoming clearer with every step closer, as though I had suddenly become nearsighted.

When I reached the split in the path, the sign came into focus too. It had the word "TUTORIAL" carved into it in block lettering. Under the etching was a map of a diamond-shaped path. At each corner of the diamond was a title. The eastern point was called Menus, the northern point was called Actions, the western point was called Community, and the southern point had a red box with "You are here!" written in it.

"Really?" I murmured, jumping when my voice echoed.

Between the surreal surroundings and the menus, I realized where I must be. *How did I end up in a Dream Game?*

Considering I had no clue what was going on, I guessed that the direction marked "Community" would be my safest bet for finding answers, so I went left. Less than a few yards past the Y-junction, an animated circle appeared before me, continuously filling up with blue liquid.

Huh . . . it's a loading icon. I heard the chirping sound of a successful Internet connection. Five bars rose and then vanished, only to be replaced with a black window that had three blank spaces for a Username, Password, and Email.

I stared blankly at the window for a moment before deciding to just go along with whatever trick the universe was playing on me. I tried to touch the window to select the option, but my hand went right through it. Remembering the earlier menu, I said "email," and the word began to glow. Since talking aloud seemed to be working, I verbally spelled out my email and password. Both were accepted, but when I tried to create a username, the window rejected it.

— Existing username. Try something else —

Each time I tried a new name, the window would shake, and the message to "try something else" would reappear. I wasn't surprised. So many Dream State accounts had been created in the past few years that it was almost impossible to find one without numbers or alternative letters. After a few unsuccessful attempts, the system finally accepted NotThatNoah.

Now that I was registered, a chat window appeared, and

an invitation window immediately popped up on top of it. I was surprised to see my mother's name followed by three random numbers. I didn't hesitate to accept.

"Noah?" My mother's voice rang out in my head, racked with worry. "Noah, how are you?"

"I feel . . . fine." I moved my head, and the window followed my vision. "What's going on? Why am I in a Dream Game?"

"Oh dear . . . you were in a car accident."

Car accident? The words seemed foreign, disconnected. A buzzing apprehension fluttered in the back of my mind.

"Your brain was damaged during the crash. The doctor says your body is now fully paralyzed."

Paralyzed.

The weight behind her words hit me in a rush, and everything suddenly made sense. My body—which wasn't really a body at all—froze, and I felt a pit form in my stomach. My heart pounded loudly in my ears as my anxiety crept in and clutched my chest, making it difficult to breathe.

"In a strange way, it's a little funny," she continued. "After all of those awful things being said about it online and all the times your father and I told you not to try it, the Dream Engine is the only thing that has the wetware interface that would let us talk to you."

My mother continued to talk but her voice started to sound farther and farther away. "Noah? Don't panic, it's okay! Everything's going to be fine . . ."

With every word her voice became more distant until I barely heard her at all.

▪ ▪ ▪

Sue and I had stood in David's dark, BO-smelling room for half an hour before I realized he wasn't going to wake himself out of his game. Or maybe he couldn't. We'd been let in by his roommate, who David hadn't yet introduced me to. All I knew about him was that he worked as an orderly at the local hospital.

As a last resort, I kicked David's bed and screamed at him. He was so far under that his only response was to grunt and roll over.

During my freshman year, I'd enjoyed playing MMO games as much as David and Brock, the third musketeer of our little group of friends. When Brock started playing the new Dream Engine, or the "harder stuff" as we called it back then, we were shocked by how addicted he became to it. Sue and I were going out by then, and after seeing how the game had turned Brock into a recluse, we were both completely against being sucked into it.

Schizophrenia, narcolepsy, drug overdoses—there were a myriad of boogeyman-like risks being rumored about online to scare the parents of any gamer who might have considered buying the Dream Engine. Were any of these true? Probably not, but I wasn't going to risk it. Being skeptical of the dangers of smoking didn't help the people who died of lung cancer.

Now that David was getting into Dream Games as well, the game had stripped me of my two best friends.

Sue's dark hair whipped around as she made for the door.

Frustrated, I stole a bottle of soda from David's bedside table. Since two were left out, I'd assumed one was for me anyway. As I left, I gulped it down and then threw the bottle into the recycling bin outside.

I followed Sue out to my car. She was sitting in the passenger seat, eager to leave, frowning at the state we had found David in. We took off down the back road, heading for the highway.

"If he thinks a game is more important than spending time with you, you're better off not being friends with him," she said as we stopped at a red light. "The last time we all hung out together was over a month ago, and staying up all night playing that old console fighting game was fun, but now we barely even talk. It's like he's slipped into a coma."

The sky darkened as raindrops began to fall, the approaching night close on the heels of the overcast clouds. I turned on my lights.

"Neither of us have tried it before, so we don't really know what it's like for them," I said. "Maybe it's just that fun?"

She snorted. "They could at least do it in moderation. David didn't even show up for your birthday dinner."

It had been a pretty sad affair all around, and it ended up just being a double date with Sue's sister and her boyfriend, who was so introverted I could barely get a word out of him. By the end of it, I felt sorry for Sue for putting in so much effort, booking a large table at my favorite restaurant, and even making a cake to be brought in after the main course.

A car horn went off behind me a second after the light turned green. The impatient driver continued to ride my tail even as I turned onto the highway. His lights were on high beam, so I could barely see anything in my rearview mirror.

I squinted, trying to clear my vision. "I mean . . . it's their choice how they spend their life, no matter how we feel about it."

I didn't know why I was defending them. I was just as

against their gaming lifestyle as she was.

Sue crossed her arms, screwing up her normally gentle face. "Still, I would never say a life where you have to take mind-altering drugs to have a good time is a *good* life. Didn't Brock tell you that a bunch of people died from overdosing on DSD?"

"I'm not sure how seriously we should take his story." I shook my head roughly, but not because I was disagreeing with her. A sudden weariness was wrapping itself around me like a warm blanket, making my eyelids droop. "The guy has . . ." I yawned. "Watched a few too many conspiracy videos. Besides, I think he likes you, and he knows that if he talks about DSD, you'll listen."

"Well, Brock said he's going to mail me the video evidence on a flash drive today. It should really add weight to my petition to get DSD out of stores and—"

She was interrupted by another roar of the horn from the car behind us. It jolted me from my stupor.

Sue turned in her seat and made a rude gesture at the driver. "What's your problem, huh?"

That's . . . a very good . . . question.

I couldn't focus on the road. With a quick glance through the rain-streaked windshield to check for lights in the darkness, I eased on the brake to take a left off the highway. I had to pull over and take a rest before I caused an accident.

Time skipped forward, and I heard Sue scream, "Noah, stop!"

I jolted awake just in time to see that there were lights ahead coming straight for us. I didn't have time to wonder why I hadn't seen them before. I floored the accelerator, hoping to cut past them. I wasn't fast enough. A truck slammed into my car. The sound of shattering glass and folding metal overpowered the car horns as we spun from the impact.

■ ■ ■

I opened my eyes again. Despite the beautiful blue sky above me, this tutorial was like a nightmare I couldn't wake up from.

My mother's frantic voice came back to me. "Are you hearing what I'm saying, Noah? You won't be able to move your body. Keeping you in the game is the only way you'll be able to communicate with anyone. Do you understand?"

"A-are you telling me that the only way I can have contact with the outside world is to stay in here?" My trembling voice echoed back at me.

"I'm sorry, dear. The doctor says your brain will heal but that it will take some time. You'll have to bear with this system to communicate with us until then. Listen, Noah, it could be a lot worse. You—"

"What about Sue? Is she okay?"

She didn't seem to want to answer me. Her silence told me more than any words she might have spoken.

"She didn't make it, did she?"

"She's in critical condition, but her brain was so damaged that the doctors don't think she's going to pull through."

My anxiety returned with a throbbing ache that, even in this artificial world, made my vision blur. I would have vomited if the game had allowed it. I might never see Sue again, never talk to her or touch her. All of the dreams we'd had together might never come true.

"No . . . no!" I grabbed my head that wasn't real in a world that wasn't real and shook it roughly. "I'm such an idiot!"

My mother attempted to console me, but she was drowned out by the memory that my last words to Sue were in defense of the Dream Games.

Chapter 2
DREAM STATE

"Noah, I know you need time to process, but I have to tell you this. There's an issue with your connection to the Dream Engine."

I rubbed my eyes and combed my fingers through my hair to compose myself. "What problem?"

"The doctor says that playing the game helps you maintain a certain level of consciousness. Right now, the Dream Engine is the only thing keeping you as alert as you are. We were lucky that it connected at all."

"So, I'm under the influence of DSD now?"

"That's right. The doctor said that keeping your brain active will help heal the part that controls motor function. The problem is that the system is designed so that when you lose or are defeated, you are given a jolt to wake up from the trance that the Dream State Drug puts you in." She paused for a moment, as though she was building up the courage to say something. "The doctor thinks that . . . because of the areas of the brain that were damaged . . . if this happens . . . there's a chance you could slip into a coma."

Still processing the news about Sue, I found trying to decipher my mother's meaning difficult.

"You're telling me that if I lose in the game," I said slowly, "I might slip into a coma . . . and lose contact with the outside world?"

"That's right. We weren't sure if the tutorial stage alone would keep your brain active enough, so your father and I put some money together and hired a professional to train you. He will also act as your bodyguard until you get the hang of it. He works for the Wona Company and is apparently very good."

My friend Brock used to work for the Wona Company too. Players like him were paid by the company to stay in-game for long periods of time, usually drugged out of their minds. The longer Brock was drugged up, though, the more paranoid he got. He became convinced that Wona was after him, but still spent most of his time in the game. I briefly wondered if long exposure to the drug would start to mess with my brain as well.

"Is he Hero rank?" I recalled being told that this was the highest rank in the game.

How long has he been on DSD?

"I'm sure that's what he referred to himself as." She didn't sound certain. "He's going to be waiting for you outside the first Gateway once you're done with the tutorial. At least he'd better be after the small fortune we paid."

I nodded. Only a few hours ago, I was against playing the Dream Engine. Now not only was I stuck in it, but I was relying on it to have any connection at all with reality. In the game, I could hear my mother's voice loud and clear. Was she in the same room as my body? Had she been talking to me since the crash and I couldn't hear it? The thought of the game being the only thing I could sense was jarring.

For a moment I longed for reality, for something less perfect and less silent than this odd virtual world. But when I pictured reality, all I could see was Sue's body, lying still. The guilt was overwhelming. I couldn't breathe.

No. Torturing myself over this won't fix anything. She's going to recover and I'm going to see her again.

The need to do something was almost as overwhelming as the guilt.

"Alright, I'll do the tutorial now."

"Okay, Noah. Be careful. I love you. And I'll check in on you again soon."

The chat window blinked out, and I was left staring down the dirt path. A window appeared saying:

— Community complete! Please move on to Actions —

I felt anxious, afraid. I needed to move. I headed for the Actions section of the tutorial loop. Now that I knew where I was, I was amazed by how easy it was to move around. All I had to do was think it and the game responded just as my body would in real life. For a moment I thought of my real body, lying broken in a hospital bed, but I pushed that thought away and ran to the northernmost corner of the loop.

A window was waiting for me there. It read "BASIC MOVEMENTS" in big, blocky lettering, and a chart underneath listed a few actions. Communication was already ticked off, as well as Walking, Arm Movement, Speaking, and Identification. One of the points I hadn't completed was Jumping. Assuming it worked just as naturally as any of the other motions I had completed, I leaped up. I waved my arms for balance as my jump hurled me six feet into the air.

Whoa, it's like I'm on the moon!

A moment of weightlessness at the top made my stomach drop, and then I began to plummet back down to the ground. I bent my knees to cushion the landing, but hitting the ground felt like any normal jump. For the first time since I awoke in the game, I smiled.

Jumping was now checked off the list.

A wooden crate appeared beside me with the word "Climb" glowing above it. I touched it, feeling the rough, grainy texture of the box. It only went up to my chest. I placed my hands on top of the box and pulled myself up easily enough, though I could have simply jumped over it. As soon as my feet touched the ground on the other side, a window appeared with the option:

— Next —

Having gotten the hang of menus, I read the message aloud, and the box vanished. In its place appeared a floating, double-edged sword.

— Swing —

I grabbed hold of its leather-wrapped hilt. Like the crate, it was solid and heavy enough that it felt real. I swung it from side to side and then spun it in my grip.

I can finally put to use all of my practice pretending my broom handle was a lightsaber.

Swinging the sword was much more fun than pressing

the keys of the games I used to play with David and Brock. I was almost tempted to make lightsaber noises as it sliced through the air around me. It would be even better when I had a monster to use it against.

However, a monster meant a fight, and a fight meant danger. Maybe it would be safer to avoid a fight and try to keep my mind alive inside the game. There were plenty of things to do inside a game that didn't involve combat.

After I swung it down, another Next window appeared. I said "next" again, and with a flash, the sword grew into a long spear. I adjusted my grip to keep from dropping it. Above me, the word "Stab" hovered at the tip of its curved blade. I obliged, spinning the spear in my hand before delivering a few quick thrusts. It was more unwieldy to use than the sword, but it had a longer reach.

Could be useful in keeping more distance between me and my enemies in the game.

Once I'd gotten the hang of the spear, uttering "next" transformed the spear into a longbow. Floating beside it was an accompanying arrow.

— Shoot —

I grabbed the arrow and pulled the feathered end against the taut string, aiming for a distant tree. I was surprised by the resistance of the bowstring. I supposed it was probably realistic, but I'd never fired a bow and arrow outside of a game before. I let go and watched as it missed the tree completely.

Seems like I'm not going to be an archer.

Another arrow flashed into existence, but with another "next," the bow and arrow shrunk down into a small throwing knife. Like the sword, the knife had a leather grip and a razor edge that curved up to a sharp point.

— Throw —

I tossed it at the same tree I had missed with the arrow. This time the projectile stuck and I grinned, pumping my fist.

When another knife appeared, I tried again with less success, prompting yet another "next."

Out of nowhere, a heavy circular shield strapped itself onto my forearm, yanking it down. The knife that I'd refused to grab transformed into a metal ball that began to float in a circle around me. A blue arrow followed the ball through the air.

— Block —

The arrow turned red and the ball flew quickly toward me. I raised my shield and, with a loud *CLANG* and an impact that nearly knocked me off my feet, the heavy metal ball rebounded off.

Safe to say I'd prefer to be on the throwing end of projectiles than the receiving end.

I peeked over the shield's rim to see the metal ball circling around me again, moving quicker this time.

I quickly said, "Next!"

Both the shield and metal ball vanished in a flash.

— Spell Casting —

A video popped up in front of me. Instinctively, I

stepped back, worried it was going to come at me like the ball. But it just followed me, hovering a few feet in front of my face like the message window had. The video showed a featureless white avatar raising its hand in front of it, as though motioning to stop. As it moved, a 2D image of a flame filled the empty space inside its head.

— Think of fire and repeat the following motion —

A ball of flame shot out of the avatar's hand.

— Fireball —

Then the video repeated itself. I stretched out my hand and recoiled as the mere thought of fire caused a roaring ball of flames to fly from my open palm, the crackling heat scorching a nearby bush.

"Whoa!" I jerked my hand back down.

That was going to take some getting used to. In all the games I'd played before, I'd had to use keys to trigger a spell. While I had experienced walking and jumping in real life, fireballs had never burst out of my hands before.

The video changed.

— Think of lightning and repeat the following motion —

Below the text, the avatar raised its hand, and a fork of lightning appeared inside its head.

I raised my arm. A blinding flash burned my eyes as a bolt of electricity shot down from the sky, leaving the ground right in front of me blackened. To aim the lightning farther away, I focused on a distant tree and tried again. This time the bolt of lightning set the tree aflame.

Okay, I've got this. The different hand gestures were going to be a huge help. If it was just the thought that triggered the spell, it would've been a lot harder to control my abilities.

The next movement showed the avatar extend its arms forward, palms up, then quickly sweep its arms upward. Thinking of dirt, I copied the motion. A wall of earth rose in front of me.

It crumbled as the next instructional window appeared. I laughed as I used a sweeping hand gesture and sent a blast of wind in the direction of a grove of trees. Leaves and twigs went flying. I waited for the next window to pop up, but it seemed that this was the last spell to be shown on the instruction video.

— Actions complete! Move on to Menus —

With the second part of the tutorial finished, I continued down the path to the third and final part of the diamond-shaped pathway, the one I was expecting to be the most boring. As I walked, the destruction I had caused to the surrounding bush vanished behind me, my magical onslaught of little consequence to this place.

Four menus popped up around my line of sight as soon as I reached the corner.

— Status — — Items — — Abilities —
— Key Triggers —

As soon as the word "status" crossed my lips, the window expanded. The menu was gray, deactivated during the tutorial, but I could still make out the various stats. The top section was labeled Visible and had bars for my Hit Points, Mana for spells and abilities, and a Stamina gauge. Below that was a section labeled Invisible. I assumed those stats couldn't be seen by other players. They were represented with symbols: a sword for strength, a shield for defense, a boot for speed, and a downward-pointing arrow for weight.

On the left side of the Invisible section were a flame and a snowflake. I thought that perhaps these represented the strength of my fire and ice magic, but considering there were no icons for the other spells I had used, this was only a wild guess. At the bottom of the menu were icons for the status effects of weapons and armor that I would eventually be able to find in-game.

I called up the Items menu next. As expected for the beginning of the game, it was empty, so I closed it and checked the abilities menu. It was filled with the four tutorial spells I had already used: Fireball, Lightning Strike, Earth Mold, and Wind Blast.

The last menu, Key Triggers, was the smallest, which would be handy during a fight. The other menus blocked my vision when they were fully expanded, but the Key Triggers menu would be needed when fighting enemies. I used my finger to drag some of the mock abilities from the larger menu, quickly filling up spell slots with the limited number of spells available. I hoped that eventually I'd be able to add more, since four spells wasn't going to cut it once I started gaining new skills.

With the spell slots filled, I tossed in a sword and one

of the throwing knives for the equipment. There weren't any items or abilities to add in yet. I assumed jumping and interacting with the weapons were automatic.

Once I had filled out the Key Triggers, another Next popped up.

When I read it aloud, a video window appeared showing a player using their Skill Points to increase their Hit Points, Mana, Stamina, and other stats.

So, you raise your stats with these Skill Points instead of leveling?

Experimenting with the drag function, I used the initial Skill Points provided to decrease my weight, allowing me to jump even higher. However, as fun as it was to propel myself into the air, the graphics in the tutorial didn't allow me to see very far past the trees. All I could see were uniform fields that blurred into the distance.

I quickly realized that doing all this would be a lot more enjoyable while actually playing the game, so I closed the menu.

Another message unraveled across my vision with a trumpeted fanfare:

—Tutorial complete! Please choose your Niche—

My friend Brock had told me that you had to choose one of four specialty Niches. Each of the Niches could utilize every skill, but the Niche you chose determined how many Skill Points you gained for any given stat. Although nothing stopped a Heavy from raising his magic stat, or Spellcasters from increasing their strength stat, the boost of Skill Points given to particular Niches at the end of each dungeon created an incentive for them to favor certain stats and abilities.

A window appeared listing all the Actions I had learned, separated into four columns, one for each Niche. The Warrior column was mostly basic movement and melee weaponry. The Range Niche focused on the bow and throwing weapons. Heavies focused on the strength to both deliver and defend against heavy attacks, and Spellcaster spoke for itself.

I realized that once I chose this, I would have nothing left to do in the tutorial. I was going to have to enter the game. From then on, I would be in constant danger from other players. They probably wouldn't have any reason to attack me—a newbie stumbling around in the first area—right away. But I wasn't sure how long that would last. In light of the very real risk I would be in if I chose a Niche that required me to be close to my opponents, either Range or Spellcaster would be my best options. I'd had the most fun casting spells during the tutorial, so the decision seemed obvious. If I had to pick only one while trapped in here, it might as well be the one I enjoyed the most.

I followed my gut and said, "Spellcaster."

A circle of light appeared before me as a voice said, "Welcome Spellcaster *NotThatNoah!*" It was jarring to hear the username spoken in my own voice. It must have been recorded when I selected it.

I walked into the circle of light—known in-game as a Gateway—and, with the sensation of passing through a wall of syrup, stepped through a portal into the Dream State. The transition made me dizzy, and my vision narrowed for a moment. Looking down, I saw that my normal clothes had transformed into leather garments, complete with Starter-Mage Boots and other beginner's gear.

I had arrived in a town square, and judging by the

buildings around me, the in-game world was far more detailed than the tutorial I had just left. I stood in an open, orange-tiled city center. The wood and mortar buildings with tiled or thatched roofs, as well as the Non-Player Characters around me, hinted at medieval fantasy-style aesthetics. A flying banner announced, "Welcome to Galrinth." The empty blue void inside the Gateway resembled the clear sky above me. Multiple paths branched off from the courtyard, and groups of conversing avatars congregated as though waiting for something.

I took a deep breath, glad that no one seemed to be fighting here. At least I had a little time to figure out what was going on before I was in any danger.

My new Starter-Mage Boots clapped on the stone-tiled platform as I made my way into the crowd.

"I can't believe how badly you screwed up that dungeon!" one avatar yelled.

"Me?" the other exclaimed, sounding like he was nearing the end of his patience. "You completely missed the Rare Metals in the Penance Mines!"

"Ignore them," a man to the left of them said. "They're NPCs. They'll repeat their lines all day if you let them. I suppose you're him, right?"

I turned to see a dark-haired, dark-eyed, humbly leather-clad Warrior leaning against a nearby wall. His worn-leather clothes had thick, spiky protrusions jutting out from his shoulders and thighs.

"I'm Noah. Are you the Hero rank my parents hired to help me?"

He nodded, straightening his posture as though trying to seem professional. "Yup. I'm Datalent. It's a combination of 'the talent' and 'data lend' because, as a Hero rank, I can endow and relinquish a player's beginner abilities." His eyes ran over my beginner's gear. "Tsh, you just had to choose the Spellcaster, didn't you? I guess that's alright; I don't mind a challenge."

"Are Spellcasters particularly difficult to master?"

Datalent smacked his forehead and groaned. "The worst."

"But it's too late to choose another, right?" After how much fun I was having casting spells in the tutorial, I didn't really want to switch.

He nodded and pushed away from the wall, gesturing me on with the wave of two fingers. I followed down the Galrinth road, between rows of shops and orange tiles under a clear sky.

"As virtual worlds go, this place is pretty impressive."

"Tsh, Galrinth is as plain as a bread sandwich compared to some of the other areas in the Dream State." Datalent tilted his head, looking at me over his shoulder. "It's designed to keep players from being overstimulated upon first entry."

The sound of the bustling crowd and striking hammers from the nearby smithies we passed felt right out of a movie. Even the artificial sweat and market spices perfumed the warm air.

"What's first?" I asked.

"I've got enough Moola from your parents to trade with, but we won't want to spend all of it right away. The way the game mechanics work is that you have to accomplish certain requirements or quest criteria to be able to equip certain weapons and use stronger abilities."

"Moola?" I asked. "Is that this game's currency?"

"Wona wanted old slang to be the world's language here."

A bell chimed as we entered a nearby items store. It featured a wooden floor and wooden walls and was relatively vacant in comparison to the others on the street. We began looking around the rows of weapons on display as the eyes of the attendant NPC followed us around the room. I could see right away why the place was empty. Everything on display looked rough at best; only a few items were of above-average quality.

"If my parents gave you money to get the best starter items, why are we looking at crappy weapons like these?" I fingered a rusted blade.

Datalent smirked. "That's the first mistake all of you rich newbies make. You spend all your money on the prettiest weapons. Then when it breaks in the first few hours, you complain about how much it costs to mend because you haven't built up the Forging Skill yet. By starting off with these kinds of weapons, you can build it up very quickly and easily."

"But . . . a Copper Sword?"

Datalent pulled out a worn blade from the wooden rack that was tarnished and bent like a question mark. "Copper is the best starter sword as it only takes a moment to fix and it will help you level up. Once you've learned to fix weapons, it will save you a lot of Moola later on in the game." He presented the sword to the vacant-eyed store owner and handed over a coin. "This way when you move on to Spellcaster staves or wands or whatever, you can spend more money on spell upgrades, abilities, or experience boosters. But for now, yes, we start with this piece of crap."

After we walked out of the store, he threw the sword to me, and a menu window opened to showcase its predictably terrible specs. All were low, except for its high repairability. I could definitely see the method to his madness. It was the "buy a man a fishing rod rather than a fish" approach. Nevertheless, I couldn't help but sigh at how incredibly shabby it looked.

Hopefully Datalent's advice doesn't kill all of the fun this world has to offer.

I tried to equip it but found I couldn't. "Hey, why can't I use this thing?"

"Have they really not added that to the tutorial yet?" Datalent rolled his eyes. "All weapons have to be slotted into your Key Triggers for you to equip them. Like your spells and abilities, the number of weapons you can use without accessing your main menu is limited by your Key Triggers."

"That sounds really limiting," I said, trying to figure out how to put the sword into my Key Triggers.

"It's supposed to be. Otherwise you could just stack your abilities and be OP in the first week." Datalent sighed as he saw the confused look on my face. "Don't try to put the thing itself into your Key Triggers. Drag it down from your equipment in your main menu."

I accessed my main menu, saw the copper sword in my equipment, and dragged it into one of my Key Trigger equipment slots. At this stage, I had all six available. I still didn't have anything to put in the abilities or items slots.

"Now that we have a sword to work on, the next step is to find a Rock Demon or some other weak monster to break it on." He started down the road, and I followed after him again. "When we were first talking, I coded the beginner spells into your menu. Have you put them in your Key Triggers yet?"

I raised an eyebrow at him. "You've been with me since the time I arrived. Does it look like I've done it?"

"I can't see your menu, idiot."

Well, how was I supposed to know that?

Datalent shrugged. "If you want to last in this game for more than a day, you're going to have to learn to quickly choose your Key Triggers before you get into a battle. Otherwise, you'll have no abilities to protect yourself. Not a very good situation for someone like you from what I've been told."

"So, you know about my condition then? I have to say I'm a little nervous about all this, but you're here to protect me, right?"

"Yup, that's why your parents paid Wona so much. For a game that involves a lot of trial and error by learning from dying, it's going to take a lot of Moola to keep you alive while we're training. Honestly, you're going to have to listen to me very closely if you want to survive in this place."

Datalent's matter-of-fact tone was grating, considering how real this risk was for me. But if I was going to have any freedom of exploration in this game, I would have to gain more experience, and Datalent was my only method of doing that safely.

While I listened, I opened up my Key Triggers. The mock abilities I'd added before had vanished, leaving all six spots open. Apparently even as a Spellcaster, you didn't start out with the basic spells. I shifted the abilities Datalent had already endowed me with into my Key Triggers. They were the same four spells I learned in the tutorial. With the amount of time I'd had in the game, they were probably the only ones I could use now anyway. I guessed that I would be able to use other spells when I completed some quests in the world, like one of the water dungeons would give me a water spell or something like that.

"So, I can use Moola to buy abilities, weapons, and armo—"

"Tsh, you won't need armor yet."

"Right . . ." I was skeptical but took his word for it. After all, from what my mother said, he was being paid a lot of money to advise me through this game. "But there are specialty weapons for different Niches, right?"

"That's true," Datalent said.

We moved through the crowd to the edge of Galrinth. The large wall that surrounded the entire city led out to a drawbridge that looked to be the exit. The crenulations at the top confirmed that Galrinth was definitely pushing for the medieval fantasy look. I felt a thrill at the hope that other cultural influences would be more prevalent in other places in the Dream State. Maybe a place up high with a good view of the world.

We stopped as we reached the city limits, and a Leave Galrinth option was automatically added to my Key Triggers underneath my four sub-menus.

"There are a few specialty weapons," Datalent said, "that give you crossover abilities like bows or swords that increase the distance and strength of your magical attacks. Then again, those cost a lot of Moola. So, are you ready to enter the field?"

The question was obviously rhetorical, considering he would know better than I would, but I nodded anyway. We entered into the Galrinth Fields. Oceans of grass, horizons filled with trees, and a striking lake that cut through the distant hills flashed into existence as if to greet us. Birds flew in the sky, and I could see even larger creatures higher up, some with players riding them. If I was impressed with the vastness of the orange-tiled city, I was in awe of the beauty radiating from the romanticized landscape. I sighed.

Man . . . I should show this to Sue.

I bit my lip, my shoulders slumping as I remembered that I couldn't.

Who am I kidding? She would be upset with me for letting myself be sucked into the game so quickly.

Datalent appeared beside me. "Don't wet yourself now."

I laughed as we made our way across the grass. "Even if I did, I probably have a catheter to stop me from making a mess."

"Lucky you." His voice was thick with dry sarcasm. "Either way, be cautious but have fun. After all, why else did you decide to play?"

"It was either this or remain in the tutorial to sulk."

He shrugged. "It seems you made the right decision, then."

Chapter 3
WIDOWS' FOREST

The grass was soft beneath our feet, the green Galrinth Fields spreading out in all directions. Every now and then, the sun would go behind a cloud, casting shadows over the distant hills and valleys.

"Datalent?"

"Just call me Data."

"Data, then. Where exactly are we going?" I was hoping it was somewhere a bit more exciting than this field. The landscape was so numbingly boring, I began to wonder whether I was sensing the game or my hospital bed. I shook my head. My thoughts had run away with me again, and I needed to think about something more than what was going on in the real-life hospital. After everything I'd heard about how fun this place could be, I was eager to find out for myself what all the hype was about.

"Widows' Forest, just over there." He pointed across the grasslands to a forest in the distance, separated from us by only a lake, a few trees, and half a dozen miles.

Our first landmark was a wide bridge, and the realism

of the river that flowed under it was enough to impress me. Having once been a keen gamer before the Dream Engine was invented, I was blown away by the beautiful graphics.

After about half an hour of talking, I could tell that Datalent wasn't just a good player, but—judging by the passion behind his words—a bit of a geek as well. He used most of the time we were walking to explain the game mechanics, and the bright, animated tone in his voice made me wonder whether he had once been a sales rep for the Wona Company. He showed me his equipment and patiently ran through a list of which items I could synthesize to make a weapon that would benefit me as a Spellcaster, and the ones I didn't need to bother with.

"My gear for instance." He pointed to the thick, dark-gray leather covering his shoulders and chest that thinned out and became tighter around his waist. The same thick leather continued down over his beltline in shell-like protrusions. "This is Rhino Leather. I had to get it from the Primatier monsters on the Onjira Plains. It's incredibly tough, and players need a high level of strength to wear it. So much strength that it's practically useless for your Niche."

"So, what would be the best garments for a Spellcaster?"

He grinned as though he was expecting the question. "That's why we're heading into Widows' Forest. The best beginner Spellcaster starter robes are made from Arachnid Silk. If we can spend a few hours cutting through the monsters in there, we'll be killing two birds with one stone."

Something in his words struck a chord in me. "Arachnid . . . that sounds like—"

"We're going to be fighting spiders, Noah, really big spiders. I hope you're not an arachnophobe."

"I'm not."

Sue usually picked them up and threw them outside, afraid that I would squash them.

I had a suspicion it wasn't going to be as easy as dealing with spiders in real life.

The artificial sunlight in the fields dimmed as we advanced toward the ominously dark, web-strewn forest. As soon as we approached the trees, the sky automatically darkened, and a full moon appeared high above us.

Great. The forest has a horror-movie theme.

The spiderwebs everywhere made this obvious. Soft, ambient music that I hadn't even registered until now suddenly switched to a minor key. Knowing how cautious I would need to be to survive here, the music only reminded me of the very real danger I was in.

"How familiar are you with this place?" I asked, but Data remained silent.

Despite my growing anxiety, I was impressed with the detail of the forest, from the flaking bark on the trees to the feeling of prickling needles on my skin. Even my avatar's reaction to the roots rang true as I lost my footing and my vision tilted. I was forced to regain my balance.

"Watch it!" Data hissed. He stepped over a large root and brushed a veil of spiderwebs aside as he led the way through. "And to answer your question, there's no good reason for a Warrior class to hang around for long, considering the main items you get here won't help us. I usually just walk straight through. I suggest you keep your eyes up; Arachnids can drop down from the trees."

I looked up. I could only just see above our heads due to the thickness of the pine tree branches. Cobwebs filled the natural canopy, the scent of pine a lot more authentic than any air freshener I'd smelled. We moved further in, and the roots began to spread out to form a wide path. I kept my eyes open, looking for anything resembling a spider. The moonlight shining through the needled branches cast sinister-looking shadows that made me jump. We walked through undisturbed, but the lack of enemies made the forest even more terrifying due to the sheer suspense.

This is just a game, I kept reminding myself.

Thankfully, we arrived in an area where the trees were more spaced out, the artificial moonlight shining into a large, oval-shaped glade. It was completely empty, except for the wind-bent grass.

Datalent stopped and pulled the cork out of a water-droplet-shaped bottle he had pulled from his rucksack. He waved it about in the air around us.

"What's that?"

"I did some reading on how to draw out the Arachnid monsters. Turns out you get the best haul from using a special pheromone item." He corked the bottle and put it away. "It took me a while to find it because I've never had to use it before. I'm hoping it's not too powerful."

My gut clenched in fear. "Why?"

"Because if it is, we might draw out too many of them, or . . ." He grinned. "A Mother Spider."

Considering I'll go into a coma if they kill me, Data doesn't sound very worried.

I saw swift movement from the edge of the clearing and equipped the Copper Sword that Data had bought for me.

He looked over his shoulder, and his eyes narrowed. "Focus on your magic for now. If you use the blade first, it'll break too early, and you'll be screwed."

I felt wildly underprepared for this fight. No wonder most newbies died a lot when they first started.

He equipped two symmetrical, golden-laced, dual-wielding swords, spinning them as they appeared in his hands. "Leave the outliers to me. You stay in the middle and give cover fire. Use the blade if any get too close, but other than that, your Fireball spell will be your best option."

I nodded, moving into the middle of the clearing as the first wave of Arachnids appeared. Closing in on hairy legs, they looked like your garden-variety tarantula—still freakishly large, with some even coming up to my waist, but nothing a few hours on the Discovery Channel wouldn't have prepared me for. A standard green health bar hovered above each spider's spiny abdomen.

Datalent took out the first one, the large spider vanishing in a bright flash, and I realized I should be more concerned about the smaller ones that he was less likely to spot. I let a Fireball fly, and it cleared three of the smaller spiders from his path in one shot, the monsters' health bars plummeting to zero. I fired a few more as Data continued cutting up the larger ones. Every so often, when a spider vanished, it dropped a rope-like substance on the forest floor. I guessed that this was the Silk we were supposed to collect, so I went to pick them up.

Data turned to me, eyes wide. "Check your blind spot!"

I turned as one of the larger Arachnids reared up. Its fang hit my thinly robed arm. My green health bar went down by a third, and I became more proactive with my Fireballs. I let them fly, flames roaring from my hands in bright blasts as I cleared the area around me. I was surprised that so much fire didn't burn the forest down. I checked my stats again and saw that, not only were my Hit Points taking a toll, but also my Mana was dwindling from casting so many Fireballs as well.

Data rushed in and took out a few Arachnids that were drawing close to me. I hadn't been struck again, yet my health bar continued to drop below the halfway point and had turned red.

"Why am I still dying?"

"You've been poisoned by its venom." Data pointed to an item that one of the spiders had dropped. "See that bottle? Pick it up and use it before your Hit Points get too low! It's the Antivenin."

You could have told me that before we started fighting!

I rushed over to the bottle as he cut through two more of the eight-legged terrors. I fumbled but managed to pick it up. The option to use it popped up as a Key Trigger right away. I used the Antivenin and my health stopped dropping before getting to the last third. If I got bit one more time, I was dead.

I turned back and was surprised to see Data zigzagging from spider to spider, swinging his blades, making them vanish as fast as they appeared. Inspired by the sight, I started using my own sword—which took a few more strikes to cut the Arachnids down—and firing more Fireballs as groups of the smaller ones scuttled closer. Before long, I had gained enough space to take a breather, although I wasn't really out of breath. Data took something from his rucksack and threw it at me. I went to catch it, but when it touched my hand it vanished, and I saw a sparkle of light glittering around me. My Hit Points shot up and a small window appeared to let me know that Data had used an item called Willow Bark on me.

It was a good thing because right then my sword broke with a piercing crack. I retreated back as I waited for my Mana to return, but the spiders were closing in quicker than it was regenerating.

"Uh, Data?"

"Don't worry, I've got this," he said, and I watched as he raised his arms and let go of his swords.

His dual blades shot away from his hands and flew off around the clearing, spinning so fast that they formed circles of death that cut down every spider they passed.

Swords can be used as Range weapons too? Cool!

With this technique, it took less than a few minutes for him to clean up the rest of the Arachnids. I managed to blast a few more Fireballs before it was over, but with how efficient his spinning-blade ability was, it seemed like I was just wasting my Mana.

When the glade was cleared of spiders, I saw they had been replaced by an almost equivalent number of dropped items. Data's swords spun back to his hands, and he sheathed them before they vanished, sheaths and all, into his inventory.

He then gestured to the items and smirked. "The haul awaits."

I thought we would have to go about collecting the items one by one. However, they all drew toward us as though sucked in by a vortex. A menu appeared with both our names on it and the item count.

"Tsh, mostly Arachnid Silk and Antivenin." Data sighed. "If you didn't break your sword, I would've thought this a waste of time."

"What do you mean? Wasn't the Silk one of the reasons we came here?"

"Yeah, but I thought I might get lucky and get a rare area item on this mission. Whatever, though." He turned and waved, expressing his intention to leave. "At least you received enough Silk for an Arachnid Silk Robe. We'll call it a day and head back so you can have one made for you."

He began to walk from the clearing. From the shadows there was a loud thump, and the largest spider yet jumped down from a tree and landed in front of him.

"Whoa!" Data yelled.

From his reaction, it seemed he hadn't seen a Mother Spider before, either. It reared up to the size of a small pine, hairy front legs raking the air. Its pincers gnashed with slashing fangs glinting in the moonlight. If I wasn't afraid before, I was now.

Data jumped back as it bore down on him, but this time, instead of equipping his dual blades, he pulled out a larger sword with a blue blade that shone like a glowing sapphire.

Of all of the things I had heard about this game from David and Brock, one of the features that they had talked about the most were the seven rare Color Blades. Apparently, Data owned the blue.

From his retreating bound, Data lunged forward and took off the creature's front legs with a single sweeping slash. I gaped as, with another slash, he cut the Mother Spider in two. Unlike the other Arachnids that had vanished with a flash of light, this one disintegrated pixel by pixel with bright explosions that smothered its screeching cry.

When it was gone, Data bent down and picked up the item it had dropped. I didn't pay attention to it. All I could do was let out the breath I had been holding and watch as he lowered his glistening blade.

Data turned to me. "And where was my cover fire that time?"

"That's the Sapphire Edge, isn't it?"

He looked down at the blade and frowned. "Yeah . . . you weren't supposed to know what that was."

"Why did you use it?"

"Instinct. That spider just came out of nowhere."

Silence pervaded the clearing. Data returned his one-of-a-kind weapon to his inventory.

I shook my head. "So . . . I suppose you don't want me to say anything?"

He grinned and turned to leave the forest. "If I were you, I wouldn't. Come on, let's get out of here."

Wait . . . was that meant to be a threat?

As we made our way back to Galrinth, I couldn't help but think so.

Chapter 4
BASETIER

Once we were back under the clear skies of Galrinth, Datalent led me to the Synth Square, where I could get the Silk turned into a robe. The Square was actually a big, turquoise- and white-tiled circle surrounded by tall limestone buildings and beautiful gardens. He gestured me inside a weaver's store while he waited outside. I looked around at the colorful fantasy garments hanging on the dark, wooden walls.

Considering the Silk was white, I was surprised that the female NPC behind the counter gave me the option to change the hue of the robe to whatever shade I wanted. I thought black would have been a good color for fighting at night, but after seeing how awesome Data's Sapphire Edge was, I went with a navy blue instead.

"Alright, with that you shouldn't die too easily." He was waiting for me outside the weaver's quarters of the Synth Square. "At least not in any of the Basetier dungeons."

"Base . . . tier?" I asked.

He gave me a look and began to laugh, leaning against the wall. "Let me get this straight. You know about the seven

Color Blades, but you don't know about the tiers?"

I rolled my eyes. "Enlighten me, then."

"Well, as you've probably noticed, there are no difficulty settings in this game, and Skill Points aren't good for anything but leveling up your stats and allowing you to access different weapons, spells, *and* higher tier dungeons. So . . ." He stood straight and pointed a finger to the clear sky. "For those who want to gain experience faster or get rarer items, they need to go to different tier dungeons, generally with a party. The other tiers are Primatier, Secotier, and finally, Tertiatier, the only place in the Dream State where your items can be stolen from you if you're defeated. I've heard your avatar can be destroyed there as well, but that's never happened to me before."

He began walking, and I followed him down the street. I had no idea where we were heading now, but with a sword like the Sapphire Edge in his possession, as well as my parents' Moola, I had a feeling I was pretty safe with Data.

As we walked, we passed a lot of avatars. Some of the players in the crowd looked like they had altered theirs to look like other fantasy races. Elves and barbarians were two very popular choices.

"Was Widows' Forest an example of a Basetier dungeon?" I asked.

"Yup, but it's one of the harder ones on this tier, so don't feel too bad about it." This seemed like an uplifting statement, until Data followed it up with, "But if I wasn't with you, you definitely would've died."

He said this as though it wasn't obvious enough already.

This talk of tiers got me thinking. What tiers would David and Brock be on now? Would they even visit the lower tiers after how long they had been playing? David could still be in the game from the night I visited him. How long had he spent without returning to reality? How long would I be leaving reality for?

Sue might be dead by the time I wake up. The idea tore at my heart. I might never see her smiling face again. One of the reasons I hadn't started playing Dream Games was to spend more time with her.

We had first met during our home economics class. Sue liked to cook stews and soups because it made her feel like a witch stirring a boiling cauldron. She would always make a mess, and the teacher sometimes blamed me, her partner in crime. Although there were much tougher guys in the class, she would ask only me to open jars of garlic and preserves for her, even when I was partnered with Brock. He would always give me a cheesy grin, his eyebrows moving up and down suggestively.

The memory made the cold feeling of anxiety rise in my chest again, and I gripped the front of my robe. *Will that be all that Sue becomes to me? Painful echoes of fond memories?*

"You know, if you just accepted their conditions, they would give you the rank," a distant voice said.

"Where's the fun in that?" a sly, female voice replied.

"But the Moola alone should—"

"Noah!"

It must have been the third time Data called my name, for his voice was edged with impatience. I had zoned out for a moment. This was unsurprising considering the injured state of my brain, though the game was supposed to keep my brain active while I recovered. I looked up and saw his brow was slanted in confusion.

"What's wrong? You look like you've been crying."

"Can you even cry in this game?"

Data shrugged. "There's probably an avatar mod that allows it."

Data was now standing beside another player. She must have come from the crowd because I hadn't even seen her appear.

"Oh right, this is Siena_the_Blade." He gestured to me. "Siena, this is Noah."

The woman gave me a serious look, as though judging me. Her long, bright orange hair was tied in a thick ponytail that swung back and forth behind her avatar's exaggerated, curvaceous figure. She wore light Warrior gear with an exposed midriff and a plated Warrior skirt. She must have had high agility to make up for her armor's impracticality.

After she had looked me up and down, a fierce grin appeared on her face. It was such a stunning change from the cold look she'd had previously.

"Well, that's a newbie if I ever saw one, and yet he's wearing an Arachnid Silk Robe. I assume that's your doing?"

Data shrugged. "I don't mind doing hired work if the price is right."

"I don't really have a choice. I'm kind of stuck in here," I said.

Her eyes narrowed.

Data nodded. "Seems this game is being used to communicate with paralytics now."

"You're kidding!" she exclaimed, hands covering her mouth.

Data ran his fingers through his hair. "Tsh, that's not the worst of it."

"How could it be worse?"

That was a very good question. *How could being stuck in this game and not being able to wake up be second place to anything?*

"I've been contracted to give him basic training and not let him die for at least the first three days he's here. I've been told that . . ." Data looked at me then, and I realized his eyes were asking whether or not he could tell her the second half of my problem. I nodded, and he continued. "I've been told that if he dies while in his condition, he won't be able to voluntarily log back in again. He's got one life only, and losing it means losing his contact with the rest of the world."

Siena's wide eyes bugged further. "You poor boy! You can't even leave Basetier!"

"What, why?"

Data sighed. "Another thing to explain, I suppose. Why don't you take this one, Siena?"

I turned my puzzled attention in the redhead's direction.

"With every tier but this one, there are competitions held with prizes and higher ranks for whoever can survive the longest in the dungeons. Your consecutive time on a tier is called a Survival Record. Every day spent in Basetier translates to an hour that will be added to your time in Primatier. And you'll build up more time here than anyone since you don't have to log out to pee or anything." She shook her head as though in disappointment on my behalf. "But it also means that, as soon as you enter a higher tier dungeon, you'll be hunted down by any guild trying to eliminate the competition."

Data inclined his head. "It's going to make training a little more difficult, slower too, but at least you'll be busy for a while. After all, you're stuck in here. You might as well keep yourself occupied."

"Well, I guess that's just more motivation to prepare well prior to entering them," I said.

There was a pause.

Siena laughed loudly. "Wow, that's pretty gutsy, kid! Tell you what, if you ever decide to do a Primatier dungeon, I'd be proud to be in your party!"

A window popped up in my vision with Siena's contact information. Waiting behind it, with time-stamps from when I had been in Widows' Forest, were two more that I hadn't noticed before. Here I'd thought I had been forgotten about, but it looked like my mother had been busy getting in touch with my old friends, giving them my in-game contact details. I won't lie, after everything I'd been through, noticing Brock and David's usernames on the list was uplifting.

"Well now, you're a popular boy. I won't keep you two any longer." She brushed back her long, ginger ponytail and began walking into the crowd. "I'm heading to my real bed. See ya later!"

Data nodded, and I waved as she moved off.

"Who's she?" I asked.

"A friend. But even with my friends, you need to be careful, especially you. She's the type of player who tends to bite into things she can't chew and run blindly into battles. She has fun. She's a *real* player in this world."

"What does that mean?"

Data started back in the direction where I had first arrived. I followed after, keeping up so I could hear his voice over the others in the crowd.

"After I first accepted your parents' contract, I was having second thoughts. After all, your motive in the game was to survive. But now I'm glad I did."

Walking beside him, I barely felt the impact of the players' elbows through the defense of my new robe.

"There's a big difference between living and just trying to survive. When you put your life on the line and show some courage, that's when you're really playing the game. I thought you would just expect me to be your bodyguard, but going to a Primatier dungeon, despite the risks involved . . . well, it's given me another outlook on the situation."

That's probably why he was a little cold with me to begin with. Maybe he'll lighten up, and we can have a bit more fun now.

We arrived at the open square, and he stopped.

"It's coming up on four hours of supervision already," Data said. "I'm going AFB for now. I need a shower and some food."

"AFB?"

"Away from bed," he clarified. "Anyway, we'll meet back here in exactly six hours, okay?"

Knowing that I wouldn't have him to guide me until then, that I would be alone for the first time in this world, a panicked feeling bubbled up in my chest. Besides the tutorial, he had been with me since I'd arrived.

"What am I supposed to do?"

Data planted his hands on his hips and rolled his eyes. "Tsh, I don't know. Have fun, go out and explore. I'll give you some Willow Bark and an allowance of Moola, but it shouldn't be too dangerous for you in Basetier now that you have the Arachnid Robe." He looked up as though glancing at his own menu. "I would suggest getting in contact with some of your friends. I saw that you have a few in the Dream State."

I nodded.

"Those people are going to become very important to you over the next few weeks. Get in touch with them and try to remain on good footing. Teamwork is one of the most important parts of the game." He gave me a look then that I couldn't quite place, like only his lips were smiling. "Especially on the higher tiers."

The gate then flashed, and Datalent vanished. I was alone again. I recalled then that I had seen an exclamation mark beside David's contact details on the window that had come up. I found it, pulled it up again, and focused on his name before speaking.

"Hey, David, were you tryi—"

I was interrupted by the sudden voice of my friend screaming, "Noah, is it true? Are you really stuck in the DS?"

"Y-yeah."

"That's great!"

Chapter 5
DRAGON ARM

David and I had arranged to meet in the theater district of Galrinth where the Wona Company's cutscenes, montages, gameplay commentary, and new trailers could be viewed. Despite the content being less than classy, the district was created to look like an ancient, outdoor amphitheater. Unlike everything I had seen in Basetier so far, the marble pillars and statues gave this district a different feel from the medieval setting.

I arrived at the step seats of the amphitheater and saw the Heavy Niche character class that David had chosen for his avatar sitting on a step. Contrasting with the massive size of his body, his facial features looked relatively the same as in real life. His scrawny, dreadlocked head looked out of proportion on his armored, tank-like body. Dream State avatar faces could be set to something other than the user's face, but considering the reach such large arms would give him, David seemed to care more about utility than his appearance. In such a classy-looking area, his gear made him stand out all the more.

David was just as I remembered him, personality-wise anyhow.

"Noah!" he exclaimed in his boyish voice, another thing that didn't fit his avatar's body shape. "Hey man. It's been a while!"

"Funny, I saw you only yesterday."

He looked confused. "You did? But I don't—"

"You were busy, like the last three times I visited."

His eyes shifted. "I didn't know . . . but yeah, I guess I would've been now that I think about it."

He fumbled for an excuse, and I remembered what Datalent told me about the importance of in-game friends. Still, he wouldn't be any good as an in-game friend if I couldn't trust him to have my back. He had dropped off the face of the earth on me before. I'd barely seen him since he'd dropped out of school to play the Dream Engine.

Am I really so petty that I'd let our friendship hinge on whether or not he apologizes?

"Sorry, man. I just get sucked into a new game when I finally get my hands on it. You should know what I mean. Back in the day I couldn't get you away from a good MMO." David's massive shoulders hunched forward. "Anyway, now that you're here with me, I can make up for all of my neglect by giving you the grand tour of Basetier! Where have you been so far?"

"I arrived here less than five hours ago. So far, I've been to Widows' Forest and got enough Arachnid Silk for a robe." I lifted the hem of my new garment proudly, despite the fact that Datalent had done most of the work.

"And here I thought you paid for it! That's one of the harder dungeons on Basetier!" He stood and placed his hands on his hips. "It's surprisingly realistic how the weight of the armor cramps your back if you don't have enough strength." He stretched his back with a groan. "How about I take you to my favorite dungeon, then? We can take the Gateway to Toena and go from there to Mishiji Temple."

I was hesitant to try a dungeon without Data but could tell that David was trying to make everything up to me. "Is it on Basetier?"

"Of course! Seriously easy when you've done it as much as I have." He patted me on the back, the weight of his palm making me stagger. "Not like I'm going to make a noob like you go to Primatier without building up your abilities first."

"Okay, sounds good." I was nervous, but Data did tell me I should be able to survive most Basetier dungeons with my robe. Then my mind turned to my broken Copper Sword. "I think I'll need a new weapon, though." We began climbing the stairs leading back to Galrinth's main street. "I haven't really learned to forge yet, and my latest sword just broke."

"No problem. Toena has some of the best weapon shops. Besides, I can see if any of my usuals want to come along. Chloe and Keri don't mind the grind. We've done the temple enough times that it shouldn't be too difficult."

"Chloe and Keri?"

"Ha, they're my groupies." He winked at me. "Female Heavies look like those juiced-up woman bodybuilders. Most girl players avoid them. But tanks are necessary for parties on the higher tiers, so I'm kind of a desired commodity for their group. Especially considering their last tank now suffers from narcoleptic spells and has become unreliable."

"Was that—"

"Nah, he had sleeping problems before he started playing

the game." David shook his head. "You really need to stop paying so much attention to E-News. They're all bought off by the old console companies. You can't really trust their biased reports."

I laughed. "That's just like you to jump on a conspiracy theory."

"Me?" David said, placing a hand on his chest in mock outrage. "What about Brock? Back in the day, his theories made the Illuminati sound like a child's bedtime story."

In spite of our differing opinions, I grinned. It was great to have my friend back. Laughing and bickering, we made our way out of the amphitheater and into the town square.

Walking beside a Heavy really changed up the way you could travel through a town. Crowds parted so they wouldn't be jostled aside. It seemed a common rule for Heavies to avoid each other in the street, for a collision would be disastrous for everyone in the vicinity. Fortunately, if two Heavies were to fight, it would take a long enough time for the two to reach each other that people could get out of the way. We moved past the first shops Datalent had ignored earlier and climbed the steps to the glowing Gateway in the bustling town square. I didn't know how Data would feel about me buying a weapon without his say, but I didn't think he expected me just to sit on my butt and wait for him to get back.

"Have you heard of any decent Spellcaster weapons?" I asked.

"Toena has some of the best smithies in Basetier. Although they're better for Warrior class weapons, their Monks and Shaman Forgers can whip up a decent staff or set of specialty armor."

We stopped, and the Key Trigger for the Gateway popped up. I had to be careful touching the menu because the Logout option was right there alongside the Transfer option.

Among the many fantasy settings in Basetier, I picked Toena. The sudden forceful teleporting made me feel like I was being pulled up from deep underwater. My vision narrowed, and the sensation made my stomach churn.

"Hey, Noah, are you okay?" David asked.

My senses seemed to come back to me in a rush, and I had to steady myself to stop the world from spinning. I looked up at the red sky and studied my surroundings. The place definitely had a feudal Japanese style to it, from the sloping tiled roofs and hardpan floors to the kimonos of the NPCs.

"Noah?"

"I'm fine. The transfers mess me up a bit, but I recover quickly." I guessed the process of swapping the mind to different servers was a less intense version of the prompt to wake up. It was the same stimulus that could make me fall into a coma. But it didn't seem to be strong enough to do more than disorient me for a minute.

I shook my head. "Next time . . . I think I'll walk."

"Yeah, sure." David snorted. "If you want to waste several hours. Even with a mount, it would be a huge waste of time."

"They have those here?"

"Uh-huh, look." He pointed to the sky, and I saw various giant, winged monsters flying above us.

"Oh, we can ride those?"

He nodded. "Once you've passed a Secotier dungeon. Come on, I'll take you to the market square and let you do some shopping while I wait for the others to show up."

I was starting to get sick of the generic medieval-style setting, so Toena was a breath of fresh air. More than a few players walked past wearing either samurai armor or kimonos. Many of the buildings were tall towers with multiple curved eaves. I recognized them as pagodas from my graphic design and architecture class, one of my favorite parts of school aside from home ec with Sue.

The pagodas were blood red and charcoal black, with stone komainu and fox statues on either side of their entrances.

We made our way to a few old-school smithies run by NPCs. David led me farther down to an area where several Monk Forgers were crafting magic specialty weapons, a few of them sitting cross-legged under sheeted shelters around a raked-sand pathway.

"I'll be waiting for the others around here. Scope out the place and see if anything catches your eye." David waved his hand at the different stores. "All of this stuff should be decent enough for spell casting, defense, and fast Mana regeneration, which you'll need because, let's face it, Spellcasters don't have the best defense stats."

I spent the next few minutes window shopping, despite there being no windows to speak of. I looked at the mystic staves with dragon carvings and magically enhanced knives. My friend Brock had once mentioned something called specialty magic armor, which focused on multiple stats at once, and I wanted to find something that could increase my Mana regeneration speed, considering how slow it had been in Widows' Forest.

This occurred to me at the exact time that I noticed a

beautiful, all-in-one gauntlet, buckler, and shoulder guard. It was completely blood red and connected by armored plates like the shell of an armadillo. From what I could see of its Mana regeneration and high fire defense stats, it was just what I needed, not to mention it had an awesome name.

It was called a Dragon Arm.

Datalent had told me not to jump at any pretty-looking weapons, but he had said nothing about armor. I walked over to the old-looking NPC who was sitting on the heels of his feet and stroking his long, white beard. His clouded eyes gave him the look of a blind man, but when I pointed to the armor, his face shifted, and he nodded. I had a lot of Arachnid Silk left over after synthesizing my robe. I sold the Silk, giving me enough Moola along with what Data had given me to buy the armor. The old man handed it over, and it vanished into my items.

For a moment, I wondered why I couldn't equip it from my menu, but then I recalled what Data had told me and dragged it into a slot on my Key Triggers. I left my weapons menu, and as soon as I selected the Dragon Arm in my equipment Key Triggers, it appeared on my left arm.

I continued down the pathway to see if there was anything else I should come back for. Although there were a few other items that caught my eye, I felt content with my purchase and made my way back to where David said he would be waiting for me. As I left the raked-sand pathway, I noticed his massive form standing with two smaller figures. Their black-and-white colors seemed to contrast like yin and yang against David's gray armor.

"Ah, Noah!" David called, running to meet me as though escaping from an argument. From the scowls on the two girls' faces, I wouldn't have been surprised. "These two are Chloe and Keri."

I studied the girls' avatars. The blonde one, Keri, had soft features, and her beautiful white robes were held tightly to her body with warding belts, which I'd heard were one of the most powerful defensive accessories a Spellcaster could have. I guessed she would need that much defense as a supporting Spellcaster. In PvP fights, the support player was usually the enemy team's first target because their healing abilities could reverse all of the damage for their team.

Chloe had the sharp jawline of a supermodel. She had shoulder-length, dark brown hair and wore black leather garments specifically designed for quick movement. My first assumption was that she was an assassin, although I didn't remember that Niche being an option in the tutorial. Where Keri had a generic white staff with a crystal at its end, Chloe had black throwing knives everywhere within convenient reach on her dark clothing.

"Oh, you're a Range Niche!" I blurted out.

Chloe's scowl turned on me, her arms crossed. "What's that supposed to mean?"

"Well, your garments make you look like a ninja, but that wasn't a Niche option when I chose mine. It looks cool," I said, hoping a compliment would nullify her cold expression.

"Flattery will get you nowhere." She turned to David. "What's this about doing the Mishiji Temple again? We've done it five times already!"

David raised his gauntleted hands. "There is a reason for that. I mean, we know it so well, and there's a less likely chance for things to go wrong so . . ."

"So . . ." I decided to back him up. "I'm really new and I would consider it a huge favor."

"Tourist," Chloe spat.

Keri walked over and pulled Chloe to the side. She began whispering in Chloe's ear.

Chloe's eyes widened before rolling in exasperation, but then she nodded. "You're lucky, Keri thinks y—"

"Shut up!" Keri shouted.

I hoped I couldn't blush in the Dream State. It wasn't hard to guess the end of that sentence.

Keri smiled at me. "We're more than happy to help you out. But that doesn't mean we're not going to call on you when we need some firepower."

I smiled with a shrug. "Okay, that sounds fair."

"Alright, let's go!" David called.

Chapter 6

MISHIJI TEMPLE

We followed David down a red-tiled pathway in the direction of the high walls around the city, with NPC archers wearing conical hats marching along the tops. Unlike the empty fields outside of Galrinth, Toena was surrounded by tiered valleys that resembled rice paddies. Barefooted NPC farmers wearing bandanas bent down among them, not even rising from their work as we passed.

According to the clock in my menu, it had been about five in the morning when we left Toena and made our way to the Mishiji Temple. Of course, that didn't matter because this part of the map had a consistently orange sky. Sure, it was pretty, but it gave off the illusion that no time was passing. I was supposed to meet back up with Datalent in a few hours, so I had to make sure to keep track of the time. This was rather difficult considering the level of entertainment the banter between the three in front of me provided.

"Ha, I don't know, Noah. Even other Heavies make way for me," David said. "They must respect me a lot to clear a path."

"I don't think that's the reason," Keri said, her voice hesitant.

"What other reason would there be?"

Chloe crossed her arms. "What do you expect? You're too freaking big, even for a tank!"

"I'm not too big! I'm just as big as a tank should be!"

Hands on hips, Chloe raised her brow. "Of course it's because you're too big! You're our meat shield. Why else would we keep you around?"

"Why else would we keep you around?" David exaggerated his voice to imitate her, although it sounded nothing like hers. "Because you need me, that's why!"

"You really think that we couldn't replace you?" Chloe exclaimed, snorting in derision. "There are bigger, party-less tanks in this world that would be glad to be adopted into our group."

My sympathy for David was overpowered by the amount of fun the girls were having at his expense. Still, Chloe's words brought out my own curiosity.

"If you think you can find someone better," I said, "there must be another reason you keep him around."

Chloe seemed taken aback, but she just turned away with a noise that was too feminine to be a harrumph. "I guess I just like being around people that are dumber than me. I consider it a form of charity."

"One that allows you to act like a . . . . Err, he makes you feel smart?" I asked.

She shrugged. "Pretty much."

I nudged David, which actually hurt and took away a Hit Point. "Ah, at least you know you have an appeal outside of your Niche."

"What? Enabling her to be a b—"

"Davey!" Keri yelled.

Chloe and Keri rushed ahead of us, walking faster than a Heavy could. I shook my head and caught up with them as we headed up the hill.

David rolled his eyes. "What?" he asked as though surprised that they were offended by what he had said. "I was about to say a brilliant Range Niche!"

The roof of the Mishiji Temple rose from the green foothills. It was redder than the sky with large, crimson archways leading up the stairs, all intertwined with thick vines. While Chloe moved ahead, Keri stayed back with me, giving me an angelic smile to go with the halo-like radiance that seemed to emanate from her robe.

"So, how long have you known Davey for?" she asked, hands held behind her back.

"Primary school, and yes, he has always been like this."

"It's the same with Chloe and me," she said. "I guess we're both attracted to extroverts."

I smirked, thinking of the last three times I had tried visiting David. "He's definitely not afraid to speak his mind, but I wouldn't really call him an extrovert." My eyes shifted down. "I'm probably more outgoing than he is."

"Well, maybe I'll find myself attracted to you."

That shut me up.

Keri's eyes widened, and she shook her head. "I didn't . . . !"

I grinned and raised my hands. "It's okay! I think I know what you meant anyway."

We began to climb the temple's steep stairs, and the distance we had made on David quadrupled.

"I don't get it, David! Didn't you say that you like this

dungeon?" I yelled back. "I mean, you don't look like you're having much fun!"

"Fun? No, but remember how weight is a stat for armor and weapons?"

I nodded, not really seeing what he was getting at.

"Well, when you're a Heavy wearing this kind of armor, climbing stairs is as good as resistance training. That's why I love this dungeon; as soon as I make it to the top, my strength is going to be so maxed out that I can pretty much one-shot anything in the temple." He winked at me. "I may look like I'm having trouble now, but once I'm up there, it'll be like shooting fish in a barrel."

"You can see now why we weren't so keen to do this dungeon again," Chloe called down to us. She was the closest to the top. "It's not as beneficial for us as it is for him!"

"All the more reason to take Noah on a tour! Not only will this be an easy experience boost for him, but with all of us here, there'll be less risk. I'll be able to sh . . ." He trailed off, as though not knowing if I was okay with him telling them about my situation in the game.

"Show off?" Keri giggled.

"I'll be sure to act impressed," I said.

Chloe nodded. "Alright, he can stay."

I thought she might have been complimenting me, but after everything I had heard from her so far, I didn't want to jump to conclusions.

I was just glad I didn't have to explain myself all over again. David hadn't yet revealed anything I wanted to keep hidden.

When we reached the top, we waited for David to catch up. When he did, Keri brought a hand to her chest and cast her Speed Amp support spell on him, temporarily bathing him in light. David raised his arms and laughed in a high-pitched voice that made it sound like his avatar had inhaled helium. He then ran in a circle around us.

"I'm ready, let's go!" he shouted.

Chloe walked ahead of us. "Yeah, let's get this over with."

Although there were other buildings in the area, we headed straight for the central pagoda, the tallest I had seen so far. We moved under a massive red archway and into a long corridor. The Mishiji Temple used traditional Asian aesthetics on a much larger scale. I stopped and stared up in awe at an opening in the ceiling that expanded through every floor, right up to the top of the towering temple. Spiraling stairs wound up high above us, their walls crowded with terra-cotta statues.

Three katana-wielding skeletons in samurai armor charged at us. David laughed like a kid in a playground and advanced on them in turn, shattering their bodies easily with broad sweeps of the mace he had equipped.

Chloe raised a brow at me. "See what I mean?"

I nodded but decided David wasn't just going to take all of the experience for himself. Although Skill Points were divided among those who acted, the player who made the killing blow received the lion's share. However, those that used spells and abilities received Skill Points for increasing magic and Mana, so the support players weren't at a disadvantage.

I raised my new magical gauntlet, and it began to rapidly belch fire. These new monsters didn't fall to my barrage as easily as the spiders. Wind Blasts, on the other hand, were more effective, blowing them down like the brittle corpses that they were. These reanimated skeletons were a perfect example of why the weight stat could be a major problem for players and monsters alike. I began to hope my gauntlet didn't weigh me down too much, considering how low my strength was.

With the boost the Dragon Arm gave to my magic and David's assistance, it was indeed like shooting fish in a barrel. Then the undead bowmen appeared. Although the arrows bounced off David's armor, I wasn't so lucky. With a startling jolt, one hit me in the shoulder, sinking into my skin and taking off a decent amount of Hit Points.

They were swiftly recovered thanks to Keri's healing spell. Chloe then ran in and grabbed my arm, pulling me behind one of the temple's pillars so I didn't end up looking like a hedgehog.

She muttered to herself as she grabbed two of her black throwing knives. "Bring us here and leave us to babysit your friend just so you can rush in and get all the experience for yourself!" She leaned out and threw a knife before ducking away from an arrow. "I—" She threw another before leaning back and grabbing three more. "Don't . . . think . . . so!" she yelled, throwing a knife with each word.

I didn't want to be a burden to them, but from how she had treated David, I figured Chloe would be annoyed with me no matter what I did.

The arrows stopped coming. At first, I thought David had reached the bowmen, but he was still in the corridor. I realized that each of Chloe's knives had hit their targets. Standing up, she crossed her arms to sheath her remaining knives and walked past David.

He shrugged and waved us on. "Up we go then. I told you this dungeon was fun!"

The more we moved up the shrine's main tower, the more David's boost was enhanced. The strength boost was temporary, like the support boosts Keri possessed, and his strength would eventually wear out. The best strategy would be to utilize the time-limited boosts at important parts of the dungeon.

As soon as he made it up the next flight of stairs, David went from samurai to samurai, caving their heads in with his spiked mace.

Using ranged attacks, Chloe and I managed to get in a few blows ourselves, but they were minor in comparison to David's rampage.

We finally reached the top floor of the temple's main tower. Inside was a large open hall. Around the swirling red and gold walls were the same statues, like the Terracotta Army but of a more Japanese persuasion. I had seen similar ones on the way up. There also was a single samurai standing in the center. A banner unrolled across my vision.

— Daimyo —

He must be the boss of this dungeon.

The Daimyo remained still in the center of the hall, a large, horned helmet on his head. This one wasn't a skeleton, or rather, it didn't appear to be one. Its crimson armor covered its entire body, leaving no exposed skin or bone to be seen. It was also larger than the other ones we had fought, and instead of having its katana already out, the weapon remained sheathed. However, its stance suggested that it was ready to draw it if we drew near.

As we walked further onto the wooden floorboards,

they began to make creaking sounds like the chirping of nightingales. As the sound echoed throughout the hall, the statues began to come to life around the walls like the Daimyo's gargoyle bodyguards. It was startling, but David gave me a wink to assure me that this happened every time players reached the top of the tower.

"The trick with this guy is that he attacks only if you come near him. It's pretty deadly if you do get hit, but if you stick to attacks outside his range, you should be fine. Just don't move any closer." David caught my gaze. "Especially you. Be careful."

"Uh, okay." My eyes shifted to the stone warriors closing in on us. Coming from the walls, they forced us in the direction of the horned samurai, the one I had just been warned to stay away from. "What about these guys?"

David grinned. "After all the steps I climbed to get to his place, I can take them out no problem, but just to make sure . . . Keri, Enrage please."

Shaking her fist, Keri used her support magic, Enrage, and David let out an excited squeal. Steam appeared to rise from his armor. Using the temporary boosts both from climbing the tower steps and from Keri's spell, he started smashing through the Terracotta Soldiers around us. They crumbled to the floor, and we made our way between the ones he had knocked down. I used a Wind Blast to make the others closing in falter as Chloe began tossing her black knives at the Daimyo. I followed suit, launching blazing Fireballs at it.

The strategy was adequate to simultaneously take out the Terracotta Soldiers and chip away at the Daimyo's Hit Points. It was then that I heard the stone-thumping of footsteps coming from the lower floors. The other statues I had seen on the way up began piling into the room.

"Oh crap!" David yelled. "I forgot to smash the statues on the way up!"

"Idiot! You had one job to do!" Chloe shouted back. "It's not my job to remind you every time we come here!"

"I went up first!" David retorted. "The least you could have done is remind me! Or maybe take out a few yourself!"

I was a little concerned. The Terracotta Soldiers walled us off, pushing us into the middle of the room. The amount of them seemed to overwhelm David, but he continued swinging his mace, clearing the area around us as we flung attacks at the Daimyo. Despite how many David destroyed, we were inevitably being pushed closer to the crimson-armored boss.

As we came nearer, the Daimyo's eyes began to glow. My anxiety rose with every step we took. It only had a third of its Hit Points left, but I could tell that we were in trouble.

"There's too many of them, David! Go for the Daimyo!" Chloe screamed.

"Are you kidding me? He'll kill me!"

"He'll kill us quicker! Keri, focus your healing on David!" She then shouted at him, "That should keep you alive. Now kill him!"

"I've got you, Davey!" Keri yelled, waving around her staff.

She restored David's Hit Points. While Chloe and I continued throwing out a barrage of knives and fire, David swung a newly equipped axe at the Daimyo. Its glowing eyes flashed, and its katana flew from its sheath faster than I could follow. It only took one swing for David's Hit Points to lower to ten percent. Keri's healing spell only returned his health bar to the halfway mark.

Not nearly enough to survive another attack!

The Terracotta Soldiers pushed in at us. David's axe hit the Daimyo twice before the boss managed to regain its original stance. Keri started to cast another spell just as it swung its blade for a second time. If David's third strike had been a second later, it would have been good night for our Heavy. Its blade stopped an inch from David's face. Thanks to the projectiles and flames Chloe and I had been hurling at it, the Daimyo's remaining health finally hit zero.

Chapter 7

NO SYMPATHY

The Daimyo's armor fell to the chirping floor to reveal that nothing had been underneath it but an ash corpse. In tandem, the hundreds of Terracotta Soldiers crumbled around us. The cloud of dust swirled in the air around the room before being sucked into one of the walls. Much like when Data and I had finished Widows' Forest, a window appeared with the item count and message:

— END OF DUNGEON —

The items were mostly samurai armor that would be sold for Moola upon returning to Toena.

David swung his axe in victory. "Oh yeah, experience bonanza!"

I laughed, immersed in the excitement of the game.

"You see, that's why we don't want to do this temple every week!" Chloe yelled, pointing to her window. "Look at the difference between the Skill Points we get!"

"It's not that much of a difference, Chloe," Keri murmured.

"But it adds up each time we come here!"

As they argued, I began to feel like something was missing. I found it odd that this was the end of the dungeon. After all of that, were we just supposed to climb down again? It just seemed a bit anticlimactic.

"Why do you think the dust went behind that wall?"

"I don't know. That's just what always happens after the Daimyo is defeated." David gave me a confused look. "Why do you ask?"

I walked over to the wall and knocked on it.

"Alright, time to go . . ." Chloe trailed off. "Uh, what's he doing?"

I balled a fist and punched through the wooden plank. My Dragon Arm made it easy, and I felt compelled to see what was behind it. My curiosity seemed to have infected David, for he began to assist me in tearing it down. The two girls stepped forward, curious.

"What are you . . . ? " Chloe asked but then murmured an, "Oh."

Behind the wall, a swing bridge led across from the top of the tower we were standing in and ended on the hillside it was built against. At its end, a staircase continued up to a small chamber at the top of the hill. I was baffled that no one in their team had heard of this place, considering the number of times they had completed this dungeon.

"What do you suppose is in there?" Keri asked.

David shrugged. "Another boss perhaps?"

I moved through the gap, seeing the beautiful ribbons and flowers intertwined with the bridge's railing. "Why don't we find out?"

I climbed the wooden steps with them on my heels.

Up this high, I could make out a wall-like structure that stretched across the entire Toena mountain range.

When we reached the small room, David pushed in front of me. "Wait, let me open it!" he said, a hint of panic in his voice. "We've never come here before. We don't know what might be hiding inside."

I stopped and pulled my hands back.

"Wow, you're a protective friend, aren't you?" Chloe's voice was laced with sarcasm.

"That's only because . . ." He stopped and looked to me.

I sighed and decided to get it over with. I did like the two girls, despite how biting Chloe could be.

Who knows? Maybe it'll create some solidarity between us.

"Unlike you guys, I'm not here by choice. In real life I'm in a paralytic state. The Dream Engine is the only way I can communicate with other people, but because of my mind's condition, there's a chance I wouldn't be able to log back in if I lose. If I die, well, that means I lose my connection to the rest of the world."

I looked up to see Keri's hands were covering her mouth. Chloe turned to look at David, who nodded in confirmation.

"You're kidding me!" she exclaimed. "Then yeah, you should go first, Davey."

"Can we?" I gestured to the door.

David nodded and opened the door to reveal a smaller flower shrine inside. Alongside the shrine were two items and a Gateway. From the sudden happy expressions on Chloe's and Keri's faces, I could see the items were something they had wanted dearly.

"A White Rabbit Ribbon!" Keri exclaimed.

Chloe bent down to pick up the Japanese-style throwing

star opposite it. "There's this too."

Keri gawked. "Is that a Night Shuriken?"

Chloe nodded as they both looked back at me from the small room. Although Keri was staring at me with an open smile, Chloe was now frowning, like she didn't know how she should react.

"Let's take the Gateway back to Toena," she said and quickly turned to leave.

"Thank you!" Keri said and then disappeared into the Gateway after her.

David's brow furrowed in confusion, and he went after them. Dreading the headache that would come like last time, I followed their lead. After taking a moment to let my vision stop spinning, I saw Keri chasing Chloe into the crowd. Apparently she was done with us.

Did what I said upset her? It seemed unlike her to go so quiet. So far she'd given her harsh commentary on everything.

"I wasn't expecting that kind of reaction. Least of all from her." David crossed his arms over his broad chest. "Chicks, huh?"

"Yeah . . ."

I pulled up my menu and saw that I still had time before I was supposed to meet back up with Data. Despite not needing to rush, I wanted some time alone after spending a day learning things I would have to call upon later.

"I have to meet up with someone soon, but I really appreciate you showing me around Toena and the Mishiji Temple."

"Hey, no problem," David said, shrugging his massive shoulders. "Message me any time you want to do another one."

I turned to the Gateway with dread, anticipating the aching transfer sensation. Thankfully, it didn't feel as bad this time. With a feeling of being pulled, my vision blurred, and I was greeted by the familiar sight of Galrinth's main square. As soon as I arrived, an alarm popped up from my contacts menu. I opened it and saw that I not only had invitation requests from both Keri and Chloe but a message from Chloe as well.

I accepted them and clicked on her contact.

The message read: "Thank you. I really wanted that weapon and wouldn't have found it without you. Keri and I are keen to do it again some time."

I grinned. "No problem. I look forward to it."

Perhaps there's something to staying in this world, after all.

Her next message appeared: "Cool."

The pressure that had been in my chest since the news of Sue lightened, if only a little.

It was great having an hour to myself to explore the town. I felt that if I could get a good bearing on this city, I could begin stretching out to the surrounding countryside and then other cities until I knew every inch of Basetier. Call me obsessive, but if I was going to be stuck in this place, I might as well become an expert on it.

On my way down the street, my contact window popped up, and my mother's voice filled my ears. "Noah, how is everything?"

"Fine. I caught up with David and a few of his friends."

"That's good to hear. How has he been?"

"Uh . . ." I thought of the way the girls treated him. "Okay, I guess. I'm starting to see why my friends became so hooked on this game . . ." I trailed off as the thought of Sue returned. "Any new information on Sue yet?"

"The doctor said it could go either way at this point, but

that they are doing all they can." My mother's pensive tone changed as she continued, "Best try not to dwell on it. Hope for the best, expect the worst. I hope you're learning lots from Datalent."

"I am. I'm actually going to meet back up with him soon."

It seemed she took this as me wanting to end the conversation. "Well, I won't keep you then. Goodbye, dear. Love you!"

"Yeah . . . love you too, Mom."

The window disappeared.

Chapter 8
RARE METAL FARMERS

I circled the city—districts paved with brick, mortar, and tile—memorizing shops and apothecaries as I went. Where some of the houses possessed the authentic Gothic feel of the medieval period—complete with gargoyles and stained-glass windows—others looked a little more out of place. On one of the side streets, I noticed a collection of buildings that were more varied in height and color than those around it.

One of them was a big, blue cottage, and "ENTER TRANS-HOUSE" appeared in my Key Triggers whenever I drew close to it. Many of the avatars that entered the blue cottage resembling one fantasy race came out looking like another, only recognizable by their same garments and armor, enlarged or shrunk to fit their new body type. This had to be where players could change their appearances to suit the world around them. *Must be a good way to remain anonymous.*

I considered going in and seeing how it worked, but it was almost the time that I was supposed to meet back up with Data. I still had to make my way back to the town square.

Data was waiting for me when I got back. "You're late," he said.

"Yeah." I remembered how he had warmed up to me when I showed interest in engaging more with the game. "I met up with some friends and did a dungeon, though. It was fun."

He let out a "hmm . . ." as though wondering whether to let me off the hook with this one, but then he pointed to my arm. "I see you bought a weapon as well."

"Actually, it's armor." I held up my red Dragon Arm to show him.

"Tsh, some items can work as both weapons and armor." He scrupulously studied it. "You should have waited."

I rolled my eyes. "It increased my Mana recharge speed and my defense. I would say it gave me more of a supportive benefit than an offensive advantage."

"There are abilities you can buy that do just that but . . ." He sighed and stroked his chin. "All else considered, there are stupider things you could have bought. Just don't squander your Moola so readily. You'll need it for new abilities."

"You keep saying that, so when are we going to get some?"

Data smirked, although his eyes looked tired. "We'll need to do the Penance Rare Metal mining dungeon before you can afford any decent ones, but even before that I'll have to teach you how to reforge weapons."

"Alright, where do we do that then?"

Data took off, and I was on his heels again as he led us through the half of the city I hadn't yet explored. "We'll use one of the forges around here. It'll take some patience, but it will be worth it when you can fix your own weapons mid-dungeon."

■ ■ ■

As interesting as the properties of the different metals were, forging was still a very repetitive process. At least as my experience rose it became less time-consuming. I swung away at my broken Copper Sword and bent it back into shape easily after it had been heated by the furnace. I had to give the Wona Company some credit—being in the virtual sauna of the smithy was incredibly realistic.

"This is not as easy as you made it out to be." I was sweating from the work.

Besides the glow of the furnace and heated metal, the forge was a dark place of flickering shadows that smelled of burning coals and boiling oil. Data had to raise his voice for me to hear him over the sharp blows of the hammer.

"The reality is this: you heat the metal, shape it with the hammer, cool it in oil, and then apply the finishing touches with a chisel," he said as though it was all that simple, despite the amount of time it took. "If you have the parts of a sword, you have half the work done for you already."

"I suppose you're talking about creating a sword from scratch rather than just repairing one, right?" I quenched the copper with a hiss from the trough of bubbling oil. "I don't see myself becoming a Crafter for spare Moola anytime soon."

"If you find the right materials, you may want to one day. Depending on how much experience you have, it can be really beneficial, but you'll need another Spellcaster for assistance if you want to make something magical."

I watched the progress bar advance as I sharpened the blade to a razor edge. When the bar was filled, a message appeared accompanied by a fanfare.

— Forging complete! —

The fanfares were the one thing that took any sense of realism away from the world. I suppose the other players enjoyed feeling a sense of accomplishment, although they were technically wasting their time.

I put the sword back into my inventory and turned to him. "I'm pretty sure I get the point. I wouldn't want to waste your precious time doing something I can work on by myself. Not when you could be teaching me something new."

Something not so boring.

Data nodded, and as always, he walked off without any warning, expecting me to follow along. I guess he was being impatient with me because I was unappreciative of his extensive knowledge of weapons. I rolled my eyes and followed him out. After being in front of the hot forge, the outside air felt much cooler.

We cut through the crowds that were a constant feature of Galrinth. They became even larger as we entered the main bazaar leading to the Gateway.

"Does the Sapphire Edge ever need repairing?" I asked as my mind returned to the different weapons.

"I thought I told you to forget you saw that." Data's eyes shifted around a crowd so large that I doubted anyone would have been able to hear us amongst the rabble. "But no, it's one of the few qualities that makes it so handy."

"I assume it's the same with the other six, right?"

Data turned to me, having just reached the battlement separating the city from the fields. "Listen, you know how rare these weapons are, right?"

"Of course. My friends told me about them."

"Then what you should know is that, because of the community chat, rumors spread like wildfire in the Dream State. So, you can imagine that if word gets out that a player named Datalent possesses such a rare item, it would be like painting a huge target on my back, and in Tertiatier it's common for such targets to lose their valuable items to other players."

"But with it, couldn't you defeat anyone who challenged you?"

"Tsh, no!" Data's tone of voice became stubborn. He murmured under his breath, "Not everyone."

I decided not to follow my line of questioning.

We chose the option to leave again and made our way onto the grass plains. This time, instead of aiming for the distant forest, Data led us in the direction of some of the nearer hills. Above them were the gigantic Penance Mountains, sharing the name of the mines we were heading to. The long grass was soft underfoot as we veered off our original path to strike out for one of the closer mines. When we arrived at a line of bushes, one of them began to rustle.

Data stopped, and with a flash, his gold-laced dual swords appeared at his hips. "These misleading bushes are what we call Chaos Engines. They spawn random monsters. In the higher tier dungeons, these are all over the place in a variety of forms, but in Basetier you only find them around mine entrances. When we go inside, you'll see why."

He approached the bushes cautiously as they continued to move. A large Mountain Lion monster with curved fangs leaped from the tangle of leaves. I could hear the sliding metal of Data unsheathing his blades before he was behind it, the monster now between us. I had launched a Fireball at it on instinct. Although it hit, the monster's Hit Points were already down to zero, Data having vanquished it with a single blow. It vanished in a flash just like the spiders we had fought.

"Sneaky. You still managed to get some Skill Points by contributing at the very last second." Data rose and put his blades away.

"I need them more than you do."

"True enough."

We approached the caves at the side of the hill. The yawning entrance was ringed by boulders, and there was a rail cart reminiscent of the Wild West. It was dark and cool inside, the tunnels reaching deep into the mountain.

After fifteen minutes of walking, we descended into a wide cavern. The place was crowded with players in groups of twos and threes, each with a Spellcaster and non-Spellcaster Niche working together. Their avatars were all trolls or other fantasy creatures and were all silent with either blank or depressed expressions. Very few of them looked to be actually going through the dungeon. They were all gathered in the same area and weren't going any farther.

The calm, ambient music dropped in tone, with noticeable samples mixed in of rattling chains and spades splitting the soil. I also recognized another noise in the mines from a spell I had used during the tutorial: the rumbling sound of Earth Mold. The Spellcasters were all digging up the ground while their partners would search the piles of dirt for Rare Metals.

"Tsh, freaking farmers," Data muttered. "It's one thing to farm for items, but to use it for gain in the real world . . . . Let's move past this scum to the real game."

"Farmers?" I asked as we continued down the dirt-walled dungeon. "Like gold farmers from the old MMOs? I never would have expected that a Dream Game like this would have those kinds of paid players."

"Not by any company. But there are some decently skilled overseers who would be very eager to claim any mining areas as their own and guard those mining in them. The miners all get enough of a cut to want to stick around. They may look like slaves, but they'll be making a pretty penny from it. Some consider it a broken way to get Moola, and like with any new game loophole, people are going to exploit it to make real money."

"You told me we came here to get Rare Metals ourselves. Will we be doing the same thing?"

"No." Data's voice lowered. "If you're smart, you don't need to spend too much time going through the dungeons on Basetier before going to the Primatier dungeons."

I looked around as we began to leave the Rare Metal farmers behind. "Are these overseers any good?"

Data's jaw clenched, and his eyes shifted. "They could be Hero Class, but taking that rank brings with it a contract of responsibilities. There are benefits to choosing not to be Hero rank when you get that skilled; that's why mines are tricky. Sometimes they—"

Data spun around, drawing his blades just in time to parry as another sword appeared, slashing at him with deadly force. I couldn't help but gasp as Data's gold-laced dual blades shattered under the blow, and he was forced to jump back from another attack. The tall attacker may have been wielding a sword, but he wore a hooded cloak like a Spellcaster, and his sword was . . .

My eyes widened, and I gasped. The blade of the attacker's weapon was jade green.

Is that . . . the Jade Edge?

I stepped back, amazed to be seeing the second of the seven Color Blades in only two days, if indeed that was what the cloaked avatar was wielding. I couldn't think of any other sword that could break through specialty weapons so easily. All I could do was back off as the robed avatar leaped forward. Despite his massive size, the assailant flipped like an acrobat, the green glow of his blade leaving a trail of light in the darkness as he slashed at Data.

Data jumped back and flipped to the side, only just evading an oncoming Fireball launched by the hooded man.

He can cast spells too? Was he a Warrior or a Spellcaster? *Heck, he's big enough to be a Heavy.*

"Who's that?" I cried.

Data emptied his hands of his broken swords. "Obviously, he thinks of himself as the overseer of this place. Go farther in!" Data skipped back, and his Sapphire Edge flashed into his gloved hands. "Come even close to this fight, and you might die!"

I ran into the shaft but not far enough to block my view of the fight. As risky as it was, I wasn't going to let the opportunity to see two elite players wielding Color Blades go head-to-head pass me by.

They circled each other, both blades lashing out, although Data looked like he was more on the defensive. He seemed to be waiting for his assailant to create an opening, but the overseer must have been skilled because even when he lunged at Data recklessly, Data didn't try to riposte.

I realized then that the overseer was trying to coax him into an attack by offering false openings. Data wasn't falling for them. He must have been waiting for a spell, considering magic users were generally distance fighters and the launch time would give him an opportunity to strike.

The assailant wasn't letting up, so Data started his own barrage of attacks. It seemed that this was what the overseer had been waiting for; he lifted a wall of earth from the floor of the cave to block Data's strikes. As though expecting him to appear around the wall, Data turned quickly, but from my side I could see a powerful fire spell building in the overseer's cupped hand.

"Data, look out!" I tried to warn him, but it was too late.

The wall of earth exploded, hitting Data with a shockwave that blasted him back onto the mine floor. I could see that having both a Color Blade and the use of spells offered his opponent a variety of strategies that Data couldn't hope to match.

The overseer rushed in to stand over Data, who was now helpless. I couldn't believe it. A Hero rank player had just been brought down.

How is that possible? Hero rank is the highest rank there is!

Data recovered and looked up at the man. Although I couldn't see under the overseer's hood, I noticed how two bumps stuck out from either side of it like demon horns.

"Why attack me?" Data asked. "It's not like you can take my blade here, so what's the point?"

There was no reply from the robed man as he raised his

jade sword. Data's eyes bulged.

That's when I heard running footsteps behind me, followed by the most joyful war cry I had ever heard. "He's mine!"

An instant later, Siena_the_Blade rushed in from behind me and swung out with an honest-to-goodness ruby-bladed, single-edged sword. The strike had enough power in it that the overseer was forced back, spinning into the mine's wall.

"Three of the seven?" My mind reeled in the wake of the improbability. Then again, in a situation with two of the rare weapons already present, a third shouldn't have been that surprising.

As the overseer recovered, Data returned to his feet.

Siena stood behind him, a fist on her hip. "That's a real disappointment, Data," she said, brushing aside her long, red hair. "Getting knocked down by this poser."

The three lights of their blades lit the darkness of the mineshaft, and I could already see that the overseer was hesitant to continue with their fight now that it was two against one. Siena, on the other hand, didn't seem so conflicted. She charged in, swinging without reserve as the overseer backed farther and farther into the tunnel.

Parrying with one hand, he reached into his items with the other and pulled out a shiny red object.

Data called, "A Kamikaze Orb! He's going to run!"

"Thanks for pointing out the obvious!" Siena said.

"Crap!" Data turned to me, grabbed me by the sleeve of my robe, and began to run. "Sprint!"

I ran as fast as I could but didn't know why until there was a flash and fire flooded the cave.

Chapter 9
SIENA_THE_BLADE

If it wasn't for my Dragon Arm and its high defense against fire, I might not have survived the blast. Even with it, I barely made it through. Data resorted to using another Willow Bark on me before my Hit Points dropped too low. We were lucky.

My near miss also turned up another surprise: being damaged *hurt*. It may not have been fatal or as bad as in real life, but being burnt still stung.

Data looked even worse for wear than I was. I didn't know if he was panting IRL, but his avatar was.

"Who was that? And that was another of the Color Blades, wasn't it?"

"It was," he said, not acknowledging my first question.

Maybe he doesn't know.

"And Siena, she had the Ruby Edge. What's her deal anyway?"

Data didn't reply, but I couldn't stop talking.

"I mean she's not Hero rank, but does she work for the Wona Company?"

Data began to head farther into the tunnels. "There's a Gateway up ahead. You can ask her yourself when she returns."

I followed after him. "You mean . . . ?"

He nodded. "That explosion killed her. She sacrificed herself to help us get away, considering you had a lot more to lose. We're in Basetier, so she wouldn't have any items stolen."

"You couldn't have helped her?"

He smirked. "Tsh, I had to make sure you didn't die."

We arrived at another opening in the cave, not as large as the first, but just like in Galrinth, it had a floating ring of light on a rock platform. From the way that he was staring into space, Data looked like he was checking his menu.

There was a flash, and the beautiful, redheaded Warrior was standing before us with a large grin on her face.

"Whoa! Burning to death hurts!" Siena brushed her hair back and looked at us wide-eyed. "Hello, Noah. You look like you've just seen a rare item."

"Three at once," I agreed. "I suppose you want me to keep your Color Blade a secret as well?"

"Nah, I don't mind if people know. They can bring it on for all I care." She winked at Data.

"Now you see what I mean about her unique attitude." Data turned to Siena, his voice becoming serious. "You can guess who just attacked us, right?"

She nodded. "I was keeping an eye on him when he went after you. He's gotten a lot more aggressive over the last week. Why haven't you told your higher-ups that this is going on in Basetier?"

"I didn't know. I'll make sure to report it in my next meeting with them. More importantly, how long has he been doing it for?"

I felt fed up by their sudden secrecy. "Enough with the pronoun game! Who exactly are we talking about here?"

"The less you kno—"

"His name is Bitcon, and he's probably a User," Siena said. "Would've been a Hero rank otherwise."

This answer only brought up more questions. "Sorry, a User?"

Data sighed and shot Siena an annoyed look. "The game system doesn't only interact with your brain while on DSD," he said. "The Dream State world is only an online template created by the Dream Engine, using your brainwaves to allow you to interact with it. If you use alternative, black market drugs, there's a chance you can trigger the lucid dream-like state the game requires while your brain remains active and aware, giving you more freedom to manipulate what you can do inside the template. But using them is pretty risky. Most of the cases you hear of gamers overdosing or acquiring mental illnesses are because they're Users. There are mods to make you look different, but there aren't many other ways a Spellcaster is able to look like a Heavy but move like a Warrior."

"But why would he do that? This Bitco—"

"Money, more than likely," Siena said, but she sounded unsure. "In-game currency can be traded for real world currency, and if you can monopolize the Rare Metals, you can also manipulate the server's entire economy."

"If this is a real problem, why doesn't the Wona Company just update the game to fix it?" I asked.

Siena shrugged, revealing her theory to be a shot in the dark.

"Either way, it still seems like he can't take on two max stat players yet. That Kamikaze was an act of desperation." Data turned back toward the shaft we had come from. "Mind staying with us until we finish this dungeon, Siena?"

She moved between us, hips swaying. "You don't need to make such an excuse for my sake."

He gestured at me. "It's for his sake."

She pouted and rolled her eyes but then placed her hands on my shoulders and pushed me down the mine's path, her strength easily overpowering me.

"Come on, Noah. It doesn't look like Data needs us, so I'll show you around this place."

I didn't know if this was supposed to make him jealous, but I didn't mind. Siena was fun to be around.

We made our way through the mines. They sloped downwards, an occasional torch on the wall illuminating our way with flickering orange light.

"I heard Data mention that you could be Hero rank if you wanted."

"Is this your attempt at small talk, Noah?"

I shrugged. "Is it true?"

Her ponytail flicked from side to side as she shook her head. "I wouldn't want to be a Hero rank player. Data must have told you about the tedious responsibilities they have; they're no fun at all. Besides, rumor has it they don't have very good job security, and I wouldn't want to get caught up in any of their shifty dealings."

My brow furrowed as I thought back to what Brock

had told me of their employees' drug overdoses. "Shifty dealings . . . like what?"

"Oh, never you mind. Look, there are some monsters in the ground up ahead!"

At areas that Siena pointed out to me, I used my Earth Mold spell to bring up Rock Demons—monster boulders with stone arms and legs—that threw each other at the players. Dodging out of their flight paths, Siena cut them down with her Ruby Edge. I blew the ones that got too close out of the air with Wind Blasts. I collected the Rare Metals that had been unearthed with the Demons as well as the items they dropped after being defeated, and we moved on to the next area. I could see why Data had wanted to take me here; the value of my inventory increased with every battle.

"Ha, these guys are nothing!" Siena exclaimed.

She cut through every monster with one swing, laughing as she did it, and I would've laughed along with her if I didn't have the feeling that Data was watching us somewhere from a distance, just in case Bitcon showed up again.

We eventually made it to the end of the tunnels, making our way toward a large hollow that had been carved out of the rock. Water trickled down from cracks in the ceiling into pools at the base of the hollow. Vines hung down from gaps in the rock, where sunlight also managed to filter in. The place was beautiful in all its computer-mind generation, but it also looked like the place where the final boss of the dungeon would appear.

Siena stopped and said, "This one will take more than one slash of my blade to defeat, so I'll cut it twice, and then you should be able to finish it by hitting it with Earth Molds from the walls."

At first, I didn't see what she was talking about. I then noticed that the rocks under the waterfall looked like a large face. It had "Aemaeth" written on its forehead. Like the Rock Demons, it rose slowly from the dirt wall. Its massive underbite jutted out as its glowing eyes looked down on us, arms uncrossing as though getting ready to crush its would-be opponents.

"It's okay, he only looks big," Siena said, nudging me with her elbow. "We'll show 'im."

To put actions to her words, she ran in, jumping onto the first massive arm that swung at her, and then she ran up it to its shoulder. She jumped and stabbed her blade into the Golem's glowing left eye. The monster roared and reared back, giving me an opening to direct an Earth Mold at the wall behind it, sending a column of rock hurtling at the Golem's head. It hit hard but the jarring impact also caused Siena to nearly fall off the Golem's shoulder, waving her arms to balance herself.

I cringed at my bad timing, but Siena just recovered. "Good shot, Noah! Now we're talking!"

She spun for another strike, dodging the Golem's attacks, and I gaped at how much health our combined assault had taken from it. Another few slashes on its boulders made it lower its arms from its face, allowing my Earth Mold impacts to do a lot more damage. I must have gained enough experience using the spell during the course of the dungeon because a window popped up telling me the ability had leveled up.

— Earth Upgrade: Earth Punch learned! —

Under the announcement, it showed the same instructional video as the Earth Mold spell from the tutorial, but the blank avatar's rising hand was balled into a fist.

Eager to test my new power, I quickly opened my spells menu and dragged and dropped my new spell into my Key Triggers. I only had two magic slots remaining.

I then drew my arm back and curled my fingers while focusing on a protruding wall, and this time the stone I pulled forth was in the shape of a fist. It struck with enough damage to take out the rest of the Golem's Hit Points.

Siena jumped down and watched as the elemental being started to shake. It crumbled to the floor as its boulders splashed into the pools of water around it.

"Yeah! We did it, Noah!" She ran over to me.

"I got a new ability as well." I looked at my fist with wonder, surprised at how effective my final attack was.

"Not just that!" She pointed to the shining rocks and chunks of ore spread out around us.

I then remembered what the NPCs' dialogue had been telling me when I had first entered Galrinth. They had been talking about the Rare Metals in the Penance Mines and how they had forgotten to pick them up.

Siena gestured to them. "Go on," she said, tapping her blade against her armor. "I don't need them. They're all yours."

Like in the Widows' Forest, the nearest items drew toward me, each one with the name of a fantasy metal or mineral. I was sure I would learn all about them later while forging a Spellcaster's weapon for myself. However, as I went around the pools to collect the more distant items, my eyes were drawn more to the water than my menu.

I didn't know if it was because my real body was thirsty or what, but I realized that this was the first time I had seen water you could interact with in the game.

This feeling . . . am I dehydrated? What are they even feeding me in the hospital?

I moved toward it, cupped some of the trickling water, and brought it to my lips. It felt so real, the cool liquid feeling extending right down my throat and into my stomach. My eyes widened, and I wiped my chin. A window unraveled, and the same fanfare from the tutorial trumpeted.

— Ability to learn Water Channel unlocked! —

"Huh, I can learn a water spell now."

"Really?" Siena asked, her tone filled with curiosity. "I've never tried being a Mage before. I didn't know that's how learning new spells worked!"

She must not play with many Spellcasters, either, if she doesn't know that much.

I was surprised I was teaching something to this Dream State veteran. "I guess you learn something new every day."

"Data will be glad. The more you progress, the easier his job will become."

I looked around. "Speaking of which, where is Data?"

"Scoping the area to make sure Bitcon doesn't show up again. Considering we're done here, we might as well go find him."

I nodded and followed her out of the mine.

Chapter 10
WANTED

"Yes, I knew where to get the water spell. Why else did you think I brought you here?"

We found Data at the entrance to the mines. He was leaning against the boulders nonchalantly, ready to answer a question I hadn't even asked yet.

"The Rare Metals?"

He inclined his head. "Two birds, one stone."

I turned to Siena. "Thanks for your help today."

"Any time. That goes double for you, Data. You owe me." She winked at me. "Noah, flick me a message next time you want to do a *real* dungeon."

"Alright."

"Until then, I'm going to go grab some food. Nothing like a boss fight to work up an appetite. Catch you later!"

She must have intended to use the Gateway inside the mines because she turned and ran back into the caves. I didn't think you needed a Gateway to log off, but she must have required it to get rid of the extra DSD she'd taken to return after being killed.

"It's up to you whether you want to use the new Resource Items," Data said. "You didn't seem to enjoy forging much last time, but you'll be able to make a staff or Spellcaster's blade at the Synth Square."

"What about your dual swords that can use Range abilities?" I asked as we moved away from the hills. "I get the feeling that there's more to the process of forging a specialty weapon like that, like a Spellcaster's weapon that's also good for melee attacks?"

Data tilted his head to the side as if considering how to answer. "That's true, but let's take it one step at a time. Besides, those blades you're talking about need repairing as well. Sound good?"

I remembered the expression on Data's face when the overseer had cut through them. There was obviously more to making those weapons than just spending time on them.

I sighed. "You know what, after what we've just gone through, some mindless repetition might be just the thing I need to calm down. Lead the way."

I didn't really have a say in this since Data was already striding across the Galrinth Fields ahead of me.

As we walked, my mind lingered on what I had learned about Bitcon and his motive to make a profit from Rare Metal farming by selling them off for actual money. I realized that the Dream State could be seen as having three key goals. The first was simple exploration, completing the many quests and dungeons in the Dream world. The second was attempting to place alongside those who had the highest Survival Records in the higher tiers. The last was to capitalize on monetary profits.

By the disgust in Data's voice when he talked about the

farming, I could tell that he only considered quest-hunting and building Survival Records acceptable reasons to play the game, both the adventure and competitiveness coming together to form the world that he was so passionate about.

On a macro level, just being able to talk to other players and explore was enough for me. However, the more I played, the more I wanted to make a name for myself in the competitive arena, despite the risks involved.

So far this game has been the only thing keeping my mind off Sue.

"I want to make a melee weapon I can use magic with. Any idea on a dungeon I can grind to get the items for that?"

"You want to be a Battle Mage, huh?" Data inclined his head, his eyes distant in thought. "Well, I know a location to do that. One where there's both the materials and the Shaman Forger you'll need to make them."

I watched as Galrinth appeared over the fields. "Okay, let's go there next."

Data smirked. "Doing something like that can take days. When I show you the place, you might not end up wanting to stay there long."

"What? Is it like that desert you told me you got your armor from?"

"The exact opposite actually. A place of ice." He shrugged. "How well you'll do there depends on how you feel about the cold."

"I lived in Canada for a few years when I was younger. It'll be just like winter when I was a kid."

"Tsh, I don't think so. Extreme environments are the only places where you can get extreme items and abilities, but there's always a price in comfort you have to pay to get them."

I brushed off his statement. "Sounds fair. Besides, I want to learn an ice attack as well."

After we crossed the drawbridge of Galrinth, instead of heading to the blacksmith's forge, Data took me to the Synth Square. We walked into a store for spells. The wide room had a marble and white stone pool, and I could have sworn I heard a choir singing in the background.

"And now you'll see why I've been telling you to save your Moola," he said, pointing to the prices.

I gaped at the numbers. The water spell was fifteen hundred Moola. It now made sense to me why Data had groaned when I first appeared before him as a Spellcaster.

"Uh, some grinding may be necessary."

Data shrugged. "Nothing a few days in the Ice Fields won't fix. I think you're going to start enjoying your time in the warm forge a lot more when you get there."

I went up to the Shaman. As I approached the female NPC, a menu popped up giving me the option to buy the water spell I had unlocked in the mines. I selected it despite the high price, thinking that water would be a useful thing to control in a place covered by the solid version of the stuff. You had to spend money to make money.

She gestured me out onto the platform that extended over the fountain, and as I walked onto it, a light erupted from the water and hit me in a flash of brightness.

— New ability Water Channel learned! —

I quickly added the new spell into my last spell Key Trigger slot while the tutorial video showed me how to use it. With a new spell to play with, I copied the actions from the video and tried to control the water from the fountain, cupping my hand, similarly to how I triggered the Fireball spell, before twisting my wrist. Water rose and pooled in front of me. As I lowered my arm, it splattered back down again. It was fun to do, but I knew I wouldn't be able to put it to proper use until I could use it in combat.

I walked off the platform to where Data was waiting for me. "Let's go. After we've finished in the forge, I'm going to grab some food and shut-eye before you run off and start getting into trouble in Lucineer."

I followed him through the door, into the garden square, and down the street in the direction of the forge. What he had said made me think about what they were feeding me IRL again. Having full body paralysis, I thought it must have been through a tube, but this led my mind to yet another question of how they would be dealing with what came out the other end. It made me feel a little sick. I didn't want to have to think about wearing adult diapers while in a fantasy world.

When heading down one of the main roads, I stopped and looked around at the large Wanted signs on either side of me. They were spread out along the building walls, dozens of bordered avatar faces on brown paper.

"Oh, them?" Data said as his eyes wandered to the Wanted Boards. "Yeah, those are the ranks of the players in the upper tiers, the ones who've got a high enough Survival Record in those dungeons to be issued a Wanted rank. The number below the picture is the Moola reward for anyone who defeats them. It really is a brilliant way to cater to the competitive nature of some of the players."

Most of the avatars on the Boards looked digitally altered

to be unrecognizable. Considering how famous these players could become, they must have wanted to keep their true identities anonymous.

"Who has the highest Survival Record in Tertiatier?"

Data pointed to the poster of a grinning Elven face. "Sirswift. He's an old friend of mine, and we used to work under the same division for the Wona Company. I might be good, but I'm nowhere near his level."

I scanned the other faces and was surprised when I recognized one who was a friend of mine, or at least his avatar had similar enough facial features to look like him.

I laughed and pointed. "Hey, I know that guy! That's Brock. We were good friends in tenth grade."

Data walked up to me, his eyes narrowed, but whether from anger or confusion I couldn't tell. "Tsh, you know Brockodile?"

"Yeah, why?"

"Well, maybe you'll survive without me longer than I first thought."

I turned on him. "Wait, you're leaving me again already?"

He nodded. "I'm only contracted to protect you for one more day, so you should get in contact with Brock and team up to do one of the Lucineer dungeons." Data gestured me to hurry after him, showing his impatience to get some food. "If he's good enough to survive a Secotier dungeon for that long, he'll be able to watch your back no problem. As I said, your friends are going to be your most important asset in this world."

I began following Data again, but seeing Brock's face on the board had startled me. Sue, David, Brock, and I had been best friends for a long time before he got hooked on the Dream Engine. His withdrawal into the Dream Games was one of the reasons Sue became so bitter toward them. This doubled when Brock started working for the company that made the games. Even though I was losing a friend as well, I couldn't help but feel a little jealous of Sue's reaction to his absence. She had created an online petition to stop the sale of DSD in stores. It gathered quite a following. Heck, even I got on board after a while. She contacted Concerned Mothers of America and a few anti-drug activist groups to get assistance, and then finally Brock himself.

Perhaps that's why I was so skeptical when he started blowing his whistle.

The last time we had talked he told us he had quit his job over some dispute regarding videos he claimed would put the Wona Company under. Sue had asked if she could put them on her petition page to garner more support . . . but then the accident had happened.

He must have made a major comeback if he managed to reach such a high rank after his dispute with Wona. I would have to ask him about it when we caught up.

Chapter 11

LUCINEER GLACIER

Snow drifted down, a thick layer covering the entire town. An occasional howling wind screamed between the high, stone buildings. The buildings were unadorned, which made sense considering the fortress-like buildings were covered in black ice. Stone carvers might enjoy a challenge, but they'd have to be insane to tackle that. When I had arrived three days ago with Data, I had been surprised by the biting cold of the wind. I really needed to stop being impressed with the game; I was beginning to sound like Data.

I'd been training around the Lucineer Ice Fields for a few days now. I was cautious with my grinding, making sure not to go too far out into the snow. What Data had told me about Lucineer being an extreme environment hadn't been a lie. It was definitely a far more hostile place than the other dungeons I had been in. Not only were the surroundings uncomfortably cold, but the monsters were a lot more powerful as well.

After a few days of dodging my messages, Brock had agreed to meet me on the frosty main street of Lucineer near the main hall. I waited for him under the eave of its large doorway, huddling in the thickness of my Arachnid Silk Robe.

"Hey, Noah, long time no see!"

I turned and saw the mostly unaltered, fair-haired head of my friend Brock. His Range avatar wore light blue armor similar to his bowman from our old favorite MMO game. It was good to see his cheesy grin again. I hadn't seen him since he dropped out.

"Sorry I took so long," he said. "I've been jumping from place to place lately."

Scraping the snow off my shoes, I gestured for us to move inside the main hall's shelter dome where those waiting for higher tier dungeons could keep warm. Inside, it looked like a cross between a warehouse and an igloo. As packed as the place was, being in there with Brock wouldn't draw too much attention.

We sat in a pair of patchy seats. It hurt to recount the story of my crash with Sue and why surviving in this game was so important. I was choking up by the end, but after how close he had been with her, he deserved to know.

By the time I finished, Brock was peeking through his fingers. "Oh man, Sue . . . but that means . . . they might still be on her computer!"

"What are you saying?"

Brock lowered his hands onto his lap, and he ignored my question. "You've been forced to stay in here since then?" His brow rose. "That's rough, man!"

"It's been about a week. I assume you've been busy

as well," I said. "Being Wanted in Secotier must be time-consuming."

Brock sheepishly scratched the back of his head. "Yeah . . . well, I'm here now, so I might as well give you some hints."

"Maybe we should do the glacier dungeon here. I've done it up to a certain point, grinding the Yeti and Snow Monsters so I ca—"

"Oh . . . !" Brock almost laughed. "So you're trying to get enough resources and forging stats to get a specialty weapon? Well, considering what would happen if you lost, that only makes sense. Sure, I'll help you get through the Lucineer Glacier. Let's go."

Determined, we moved out of the shelter dome and through the snow-covered town.

"Trust me, I'll make it up to you for having to wait on me. We'll get you through the glacier, and if not, we can just use a Transfer Orb and start again."

I had heard about this item during my time in the Penance Mines. "What exactly are Transfer Orbs?"

"You don't know?" he blurted in surprise. "I suppose you wouldn't really need them in Basetier, but still, I'm surprised you haven't been told about them yet."

It is a little strange that Data didn't explain them to me.

"There are two kinds of Transfer Orbs. The green ones . . ." Brock accessed his items menu and pulled out a shiny emerald orb. "These can teleport you anywhere in the Dream State that you've already been before. Then there are the red ones, generally known as Kamikaze Orbs. Unlike the regular orbs, which you can use as many times as you want, the Kamikaze Orbs can only be used once, and they do some lethal fire damage to anyone in the surrounding area after they're activated."

"I've seen one of those being used before."

"Really? Well, here." Brock handed me the orb he had pulled out. "It's the proof Sue asked for."

I frowned. "What proof?"

He waved me off. "I'll explain later. Whatever you do, don't let anyone know you have it. Keep hold of it; even the nonexplosive ones are costly."

Slightly confused by his explanation, I took it, the description showing up in my vision:

— Allows user to teleport to any area previously explored —

If this thing allows me to quickly escape dungeons, it's going make going into higher tier dungeons a lot less risky.

Considering my goal was to get strong enough to do a Primatier dungeon with my friends, Brock's gift may have just cut my preparation time in half. Then I gasped when I saw the value of the orb: over twelve thousand Moola. It had cost twelve hundred for my Water Channel spell, and I thought that had been expensive.

"Whoa! Thanks!" I put it into my inventory.

We made our way to the black stone archway of Lucineer city. When the option to leave appeared in our Key Triggers, we went out into the Ice Fields. The ocean of snow and ice stretched out to the faraway hills. The Lucineer Glacier was to the east, a constantly moving pathway of ice and freezing water. Our boots sunk into the powder, and I knew from experience that this made it difficult to flee.

Having been training there for three days already, I was

able to show off my new skills to Brock. I'd found that I could easily defeat the Snow Monsters with the spells I had learned. One arose from out of the snow ahead of us, looking like a snowman on steroids. During my time here, I'd learned that although shooting Fireballs blew holes in them, it didn't actually kill them. The holes would freeze over again quickly. Instead I launched Fireballs at the snow on the ground and then, using Water Channel, I threw the boiling water at it. Its Hit Points melted away as quickly as its body, leaving a Resource Item called Diamond Dust.

I grinned at the startled look on Brock's face.

"And you said you needed my help with this dungeon."

"Not for these guys, but the Yetis are a different story, and I've heard the Ice Dragon at the glacier's altar is one of the most difficult Basetier bosses to fight." I pointed into the blizzard at the vague shadow at the end of the frozen path. "I haven't made it that far yet. My Hit Points just keep getting too low."

We approached the jagged rises of the glacier, the spikes of ice blocking our vision.

"Why don't you just buy some healing items?" Brock equipped some goggles to allow him to see through the falling snow. "Or eyewear?"

"Too expensive. I want to save enough to buy some more spells when I learn them."

Brock sighed. "Yeah, having to grind in order to keep up with the game is a real drag. The goggles are worth it, though, if you're going to grind here. Smart by the way, to do it in an extreme environment. It took me a whole week to get to Primatier when I first started."

"How did you do in there? Your first time, I mean."

"Alright, I suppose." He shrugged. "I was with a group, so I lasted as long as they decided to stay in-game. You could try it yourself if you know enough people. Then again, your Survival Record will instantly be high, and you'll be hunted down by anyone trying to eliminate the competition."

"Ha, I guess I am lucky to have a catheter. I'm surprised a lot of players don't pee themselves when spending so much time asleep."

Brock grinned, and his eyes shifted from side to side. "Some of them do. Either way, I would suggest avoiding the higher tiers altogether, especially Tertiatier!"

"First things first."

We heard a groan, and a large, white-furred, humanoid creature walked around a towering sheet of ice. It was a Yeti.

I raised my Dragon Arm, preparing my Key Triggers. "These are the ones I've been having trouble with."

"Then I'll deal with them," Brock said.

A bow and arrow appeared in his hand, the arrow glowing purple with some kind of magic. He pulled back the string, and the magic on the tip pulsed. The bolt flew into the beast. With a confused grunt, the Yeti's chest exploded as the magic erupted from inside. It fell onto its knees and then died in a flash of light. Brock had just killed with one shot the monster that I had been having so much trouble with. Any doubt that I could have finished this dungeon without Brock melted faster than a Snow Monster in a volcano.

"Ready?" he asked, as smug as I had been after defeating the Snow Monster.

We entered the glacier, balancing our way across bridges of ice. The farther we went out, the wider the spaces between bridges were. Water Sprites arose from the depths, their frozen bodies glistening before they flew in to attack us. I raised a hand and used my Lightning Strike spell. A single bolt from the misty sky took out two of them, and a few exploding arrows took down three more before my Mana even had a chance to regenerate.

"Is your weapon a magic specialty?" I asked.

"Something like that." He held up an arrow, its tip glowing purple. "You can create these if your forging stat is high enough. They can trigger every possible first-level spell in the game, but they need a bunch of Resource Items to make."

I remembered how expensive the Transfer Orb had been. "How can you afford so many of them?"

He grinned. "It's easier to gain Moola in higher tier dungeons. If you can last as long as I can, you can even farm there for a while."

Data had told me about farming a few days back, how he believed that people who exploited the loopholes weren't playing the game for fun and that they only cared about money. From Brock's point of view, he just did it so he wouldn't be held back by all of the grinding. In the end, it only made sense that such a market would be popular since it was so difficult to earn Moola.

"If only it were that easy in real life," I joked.

"For some people, it is."

Something about the tone of his voice as he said this told me not to continue asking questions. Luckily for me, it was then that three Snow Monsters arose from the crumbling glacier.

I drew water from the lake and flung it at them, as Brock fired a Lightning Arrow. The combination of water and lightning had a devastating effect on the monsters.

When they were gone, we whooped and high-fived, just like we had when playing soccer together.

Why was I so against playing the Dream Engine again? I've been missing out!

"Alright, enough with these peons." Brock pointed through the sleet. "The Stone Altar is right up ahead. Time to see if this Ice Dragon is all it's cracked up to be."

I hadn't been this far out before. The altar was placed on top of a massive iceberg in the middle of the frozen lake. By the time we reached the bridge that led up to its flat top, the blizzard winds had become so strong that it was difficult to move forward. If I wasn't feeling frozen before, I was now. I launched a few Fireballs to get the feeling back into my hands as we made our way up.

Behind the altar, on the back half of the iceberg, an archway became visible through the snow. We stopped as the iceberg flattened out, and Brock readied his bow. The archway was made from the same black rock as most of the town, and it had swirling markings all over and a wide, cylindrical, brick plinth beneath it. Before we could get any closer, a giant winged creature flew up from the water, landing with a thump on top of the archway. With ice shards for feathers, the enormous boss looked more avian than a traditional reptilian-style dragon.

"That's one *cool*-looking boss!" Brock said, raising both his brow and his bow.

His first arrow exploded, and the dragon let out a massive "KAAAAW!" before taking to the sky. I launched a few Fireballs, but it was too quick. Instead of keeping up my rapid fire, which was already chipping away at my Mana,

I pulled up as much water as I could from the glacier and heated it with my fire magic, waiting for the dragon to come close enough. As predicted, it swooped in, attacking Brock with a blast of freezing breath.

I flung the boiling water at it. Brock recovered and fired a Lightning Arrow. Brock's arrow pierced the dragon's water-soaked wing, causing it to crackle with electricity. The dragon whirled, one of its wings destroyed, forcing it to land. Despite being grounded, it fought ferociously. Its massive tail lashed out at us, and I raised my gauntlet to block it before letting Fireballs flare into the beast with quick flashes.

The Ice Breath hit me, and suddenly I couldn't move. Although I was still conscious, I was encased in a coffin of ice as my Hit Points slowly dropped.

I'm trapped!

I could still watch, however, as Brock spun and shot another arrow, this one exploding in its eye. He was keeping its attention while I freed myself. With my arm still in the right position to cast the spell, I attempted to launch another Fireball. It worked, and the ice on the left side of my body melted to water, leaving me drenched and shivering. Free hand trembling, I couldn't focus on the match as I went about blasting away the rest of the ice. As soon as I was free, I used the Willow Bark item Data had given me to recover my dwindling Hit Points.

That was a close one!

Despite how uncomfortable I was feeling in the chill, I was startled by a green blast from Brock. It hit the Ice Dragon, and the Ice Breath attacks stopped. Whatever specialty arrow Brock had used, it was much more powerful than his previous arrows. The dragon remained dazed and began to sway.

I came to Brock's side, staying well back from the teetering monster. Finally, it fell limply to the top of the iceberg, its beautiful scales glistening in what little light could pierce through the clouds. The battle was over.

Chapter 12
PRIMATIER

Like the Mother Spider and Daimyo, the Ice Dragon exploded in violent flashes of light. Whatever weapon Brock had used to kill the dragon had vanished into his items sack before I could get a look at it. When the dragon finally disappeared, Brock transferred all of the items we had gotten to me: a Heat Pack I could use to defrost myself if I ever returned here and a Crystal Blade that, in my menu, looked as frosty as the dragon we had just defeated. Its strength was unusually high, its durability was practically zero, and its required repair skill was even lower than Copper Swords.

"Well, that was fun," Brock said. "Should we get out of here?"

I shook my head. "As much as I want to warm myself up, if I've learned anything in this game it's that there are still things to be found even after the boss is destroyed."

I walked forward into the biting wind, which seemed to have gotten even stronger now, in the direction of the dark Stone Altar. What I thought at first was a wide plinth in the mist I now saw was actually the top of a black, brick well.

Just like the buildings in Lucineer, the black stone of the well was unadorned. The same couldn't be said for the large altar behind it, which was carved to look like the spread-eagle image of the dragon we had just defeated. On the bright side, the closer I came to the altar, the more it blocked the freezing wind. I looked down into the well, seeing that the water at the top had been frozen solid. Nothing a few Fireballs couldn't fix.

I blasted away until the ice melted into water and the water became hot enough that it melted the ice underneath. With Brock looking at me as though I had lost my mind, I continued to launch Fireballs until steam rose from the rim of the well. I cleared the air with a Wind Blast and saw there was something glowing at the bottom of it.

"Ha, there you are!" I grinned.

Suddenly my perspective transitioned, and I was looking at my avatar, like I was having an out-of-body experience. While action music played, I watched myself equip my Crystal Blade and stab it down into the water.

All at once, three windows appeared in my vision. The first showed a blank avatar holding out their hand in a fist, and a roaring line of fire shot from its hand.

— Fire Upgrade: Fire Weave learned! —

— Ability to learn Ice Wall unlocked! —

— Ability to learn Ice Regeneration unlocked! —

I grinned as I saw how much my magic-based Skill Points had gone up during the battle. All I had to do now was grind in the northern ice caves and get enough Moola to buy the two unlocked abilities. I pulled the dripping blade from the water and returned it to my items.

"Thanks for waiting. Now we can go."

Brock held up a green Transfer Orb, gesturing to it as though asking if we should use it to head back. I shook my head and pointed a red gauntleted finger back the way we had come. Now that I knew this place like the back of my hand, I wanted to test out my upgraded fire spell. I added Fire Weave to my Key Triggers, replacing the old fire spell.

Brock rolled his eyes but then nodded in agreement.

As we made our way back through the glacier, the first monster to block our path was another Yeti. I imagined a line of fire, directing it at the large, furry monster. A jet of flame roared from my hand, taking away more than half of its Hit Points before Brock used a regular arrow to finish it off.

He turned to me and grinned. "Not bad!"

The Snow Monsters melted, and the Water Sprites evaporated with each encounter. It turned out that with a level two fire spell, it took a lot less time to traverse the icy path. The only downside to casting it on so many monsters was its high Mana cost. I had to wait awhile to regenerate before being able to use it again.

When we went to leave Lucineer Glacier, a window popped up to tell me that my inventory of Diamond Dust was full. I could trade the extras for Moola and buy the abilities I'd just learned . . . or I could have one of the Shamans synthesize them into weapons.

Brock and I were trading stories as we made our way

back across the Ice Fields.

After I'd told him about the dungeon I had completed with David, Brock asked, "How is he doing anyway? I haven't caught up with him for a while."

"Pretty good. He's got his own harem, but they have pretty powerful personalities."

Brock raised his brow. "Trouble in paradise then?"

"Something like that." I used a Wind Blast to blow a pile of snow out of our way, and it flew away in a sparkling gust of flakes. "I'm thinking about doing a Primatier dungeon with them once I'm done in this place."

"What do you mean done with this place?" Brock pushed his goggles up as the mist, snow, and sleet faded behind us. "What exactly are you planning to do here?"

"Datalent told me that if I want to get a specialty weapon, I'd need to train up here. I have something in mind but won't know if it'll work until I have the Moola to try it."

"Datalent . . . that tool," Brock murmured.

"You know him?"

"Yeah, we used to play in the same party for Wona. That's until he went all high and mighty and decided to sell his soul to the corporate devil. The guy says he's playing the game for fun yet tries to police everything." Brock raised his hands in a shrug. "You think you know a guy."

"Well, he was being paid by my parents to help me out."

Brock let out a loud laugh. "What a hypocrite!"

"What do you mean?"

He sighed. "Never mind. Anyway, if someone's going to show you the ropes, it might as well be him. The guy's a slave to this game. Just don't buy into everything he says. He's a bit of a purist, and you won't be able change his mind on anything."

I nodded.

Once again, we walked back under the archway entrance of Lucineer city. Walking between the black stone buildings, I couldn't help but ponder on the different beliefs held by Brock and Data. Brock believed that one should farm if it meant continuing on with the game without having to grind, and Data thought they were just doing it to make money IRL. In the end, they just had different ways of playing the game. I wondered if this was the reason they no longer got along, or if Brock knew that Data had one of the seven Color Blades.

Data had told me to keep it a secret, but I wondered if he got it before or after Brock left his party? *Either way, I better play it safe and not talk about it around him.*

"Alright, I'm going to head off before I ruin my last pair of clean underwear," Brock said as we headed to the town square's Gateway. "You're lucky you don't have to worry about that kind of thing."

I sighed. "Don't remind me. I probably have a full diaper myself."

Brock patted my shoulder and smiled. "It was fun catching up, Noah. Make sure you get in contact with me if you ever want to do it again."

"I will."

"If I could give you a piece of advice while in here, it would be not to get a Wanted rank. For you, getting one would be the equivalent of kicking a beehive. Also, don't go to Tertiatier!" Brock walked up the black tiles to the glowing circle, but before he left, he called, "And remember what I told you about Datalent! Learn from him what you can, but take everything he says with a grain of salt! He can forget to have fun!"

It doesn't matter. My time with Data is up anyway.

"Okay, catch you later!" I waved.

He waved back and then vanished into the Gateway.

Now I can really get to work.

The Diamond Dust could be refined twenty-to-one to make Crystal Blades by one of the Shaman Forgers. At first, this didn't make sense to me because, although the weapon had high strength, the durability was so low that a single attack could shatter them. However, now that I could learn the Ice Regeneration ability, I was beginning to think that there was a reason why these weapons were both easy to make and easy to break. After all, sometimes it really wasn't quality that mattered, but quantity.

I went into the Synth Square, walking between large ice sculptures of the monsters one could face in the surrounding area. I entered the shop from before, recognizing it by the polar bear rug on the wooden floor. The NPC behind the reception desk looked like a native Inuit, his wrinkled face framed by thick furs. I gave him all of the Diamond Dust I had, and he went about refining them down into Crystal Blades.

When he was finished, I left the shop and made my way back to the Ice Fields, heading for the Lucineer Mountains.

Tall, snow-covered peaks loomed above me as I approached. I entered the dark, icy caves that led into a maze of tunnels. Because the frozen walls blocked the wind, they weren't as cold to train in as the Lucineer Glacier. Without the howling in my ears, I could also hear enemies approach from farther away.

I was surprised by the advantage the silence gave me. On my own, I was able to stalk monsters undetected. Wearing a robe instead of armor assisted my stealth as well, as there was no clanking of metal plates to give me away. Moving swiftly, I snuck up behind a Yeti and blasted it with a Fire Weave. It burst into flame and fell forward, the Diamond Dust appearing as it vanished. This new strategy made killing them a whole lot easier.

I killed as many Yetis and Snow Monsters as I could find. They had a fifty percent drop rate for Diamond Dust, so I quickly filled my inventory's quota. I headed back to the Synth Square and had them turned into more Crystal Blades. Selling off my other items, I emptied my inventory only to return to the tunnels once again. It was a long and arduous process, and I must have made the journey half a dozen times in the first day alone.

After my second day of these expeditions into the Lucineer Mountains, I was pleasantly surprised by how much my Moola and Skill Points had increased. Upon returning to the town, I invested the Skill Points into sustaining my Stamina bar so I could move quickly for longer periods of time, and I spent the Moola on the new abilities that I'd unlocked while with Brock.

As I did, the same tutorial avatar appeared showing the gesture for Ice Wall. The animation showed it rubbing the air in front of it with one hand, counterclockwise. A wall of ice lifted up from the floor like a barrier.

A second window showed an avatar doing an action that resembled someone drawing a sword from over their shoulder. Simultaneously, a white sword appeared in its hand. This proved my theory about the Ice Regeneration ability.

As I exited the spell shop, I received a message from my mother, and my heart skipped a beat. I dreaded her daily calls, thinking that this one would be the time when she'd give me the news that Sue was dead.

Please, don't let it be this time.

I selected the video feed.

The Wona Company had supplied her with their best software. Her tired face framed by cobwebby hair appeared in my contacts window. Hers was the only window I got a video feed from. Considering it put a live feed into someone's dream, the Wona Company must have forked out a lot of money for it.

"Hello, dear!" As always, she started off cheerful.

"Hi, Mom."

"It's good to see you! How are you?"

I shook my head. "Please, just tell me how Sue's doing."

"Well . . ." She bit her lip. "She's in a worse state than you, but the doctors are still trying everything they can, including using DSD to induce the trance state that might help her gain access into the Dream Game like you. However, they're unsure if she has enough brain function to be able to use it. It's all very experimental and touch and go at this point. Even the doctors don't know what will happen."

"So, at least if she does wake up she'll be able to recover in here like I am?" If it worked, I could show her around the game. I let slip a brief smile at the idea. "Okay, so there's still a chance she might make it . . . that's enough for me to hold on to."

"Noah . . ."

I raised a hand. "I know, it's a long shot. I shouldn't get my hopes up."

My mother nodded. "As long you know that it's only got a small chance of succeeding. Remember dear, hope for the best—"

"Expect the worst," I finished for her. "I know."

I continued our conversation out of formality, letting her tell me about what was going on in the real world, but my mind returned to the game.

I wanted to keep my thoughts distracted and away from Sue. While I was in here, there was nothing I could do for her, so my best option was to try not to worry myself to death and just play the game.

"Be sure to tell me if you get any good news," I said after she was finished.

She nodded. "And the bad news?"

I sighed. "That too . . ."

My mother let the silence hang before she waved through the video feed. "Bye, Noah. You know you can send me a message whenever you need to talk."

"I know, Mom." I waved back. "Love you. Bye."

The feed cut off, and my contact window disappeared.

I returned to my training with a mad fury, trying to lose myself in it. It didn't work. Being alone really made Sue's absence more noticeable. We had rarely been apart after all our friends left us behind. She was my rock. When school ended, I had no idea what I wanted to do yet, although my dad wanted me to go into finance. The only thing I had been sure of was that Sue and I were going to stick together.

I broke down in the Ice Fields, the snow landing on my cheeks like frozen tears.

I wish this game would let me cry. Why can't I just focus on this world and forget what's going on outside it?

I thought the reason was obvious: I was human.

■ ■ ■

After just a few days of going back and forth to the Lucineer Mountains, I was as hard as ice. Not only was my avatar much stronger than before, but the longer I spent in Lucineer, the higher my defense against ice attacks became.

My brain must have gotten used to the cold stimulus because I no longer shivered as much. In fact, I barely felt it now. I had upgraded two more of my spells, unlocked a seventh Key Trigger slot for my spells, and felt I was finally ready to do a Primatier dungeon with a party. Even if I wasn't, it didn't matter. I didn't want to stay in this world without any sense of forward progression, and I was eager to show my friends how much I had improved.

Once I had all of my abilities activated and had synthesized as many Crystal Blades as my inventory could hold, I decided to get in contact with David, Chloe, and Keri. It was time to try out a Primatier dungeon. Despite the risk involved, if I didn't at least try one, what was the point of doing all this training? I didn't want to drag my friends down by forcing them to do only Basetier dungeons with me. They clearly found the less challenging dungeons far too easy. Besides, with the Transfer Orb Brock gave me, I could leave if things got too risky.

I sent them all the same message: "Hey, I've decided to take you up on that next dungeon. Only one condition though, we do it in Primatier. I want to see what all the fuss is about."

David and Keri said they were available for one now but asked whether I was okay risking my life in there. Chloe said she was too but requested that I ask Siena_the_Blade to come along as well. I didn't know if this was because she thought a Warrior would make the party more balanced or just really wanted to meet her. Either way, I agreed and went about getting in contact with the red-haired wonder.

"Heck yeah!" was all I got in reply from Siena at first.

Less than a minute after I had contacted her, Siena was standing right next to me on the snow-covered streets, so she might have been tracking me somehow, if that was possible for someone who wasn't a Hero rank. Being a part of the company that runs the game, Data had been tracking my position. She must have used some form of plug-in software to do this.

When she appeared outside in her skimpy armor, I shivered, my menu shaking in a red haze. I felt cold just looking at her. "How did you . . . ?"

"But on one condition!" she said.

"Wait, what condition?"

"I get to choose the Primatier dungeon we go to. There have been a few new ones I've been wanting to try, okay?"

"Okay." I had no specific dungeon in mind anyway. "So, where do we go to get there? Because that's where I'll tell the others to meet up."

"Yarburn."

"Yarburn, okay."

I looked at the options in the Gateway menu and found Yarburn near the bottom. After spending nearly a week in a frozen wasteland, the town that appeared around me gave the impression of being in the Bahamas: wooden houses, palm trees, and sand. The palm fronds around the village led up the hills into a thick, tropical rainforest, making the area feel more like an island than the peninsula the map showed it to be. The sound of calling seagulls and crashing waves filled the background. Crowds swamped the streets, leading me to suspect that players saw it as a vacation setting.

It was nice to be out of the cold, but for me, it felt humid. When the artificial sun hit me, I suddenly remembered what I had been missing out on.

"Phew, it's hot." I wiped the sweat already beading on my brow. "Alright, I'll message the rest to meet us at the edge of town."

Chapter 13
CHAOS ENGINE

Sitting on a wall bench at the edge of Yarburn, I let out a heavy, satisfied sigh. I had a few minutes to myself while we waited for everyone. As the others got ready for our expedition, I took the time to gather my nerve. A week ago, I would've been hesitant to even go out into the world without Datalent there to guide me. There was always a chance that I would be attacked by another player.

What Data said was right; there really is a big difference between playing the game and just surviving in it.

As I waited, I watched the giant flying mounts shoot into the sky and come in to land and wondered when I would be able to get one of those to fly around on. After hearing about the guilds from Siena, I could only guess what other kinds of guilds there were. Maybe there was even a Flying Guild.

David showed up first with his Heavy armor equipped with shoulders that, on his real body, would have looked much too big for him.

"You look ridiculous."

David smirked. "You won't be saying that when my high

defense is saving your butt against an enemy Heavy."

"That's until you find a Heavy who's been Enraged," Chloe added as she walked up to us, "and you can't run away because your armor is slowing you down." She'd proven in the last dungeon that she had good speed and stamina stats.

"Oh, whatever!" David spun, nearly knocking her over with one shoulder. "If that happens, I'll just unequip it. It only takes a second of concentration."

"It only takes *a second*," I made air quotes with my fingers, "for an Enraged beast to catch you, unless I'm mistaken that the spell increases both strength and speed?"

"And my armor will protect me until I'm done! Jeez guys, it's like you think I'm Sirswift or something!"

Chloe snorted. "Don't flatter yourself. That's like comparing a professional choir to someone singing in the shower."

Keri arrived just in time to back him up and sat beside me. "He's right though, it's not like I'm going to let a teammate get killed when he's mid-menu. What kind of White Mage would I be?"

"A White Mage who cares more about keeping the Spellcaster alive," David murmured, his eyes drifting to me.

"What's that supposed to mean?"

David raised gauntleted hands. "Well, considering we know what would happen to you if you got taken out, it's only natural that Chloe and Keri's priorities would be skewed toward you."

Chloe smirked. "My mom always told me not to neglect my vegetables."

"Hey! I'm not a vegetable; it was only the part of my brain that controls motor function that got damaged."

Chloe shrugged. "Same thing."

"Guys!" A voice groaned above us. "Are we going to get out there or just talk about it?"

I looked up and then jerked my head down quickly, realizing I had almost glanced up Siena_the_Blade's Warrior skirt. She grinned at my instinctive modesty and leaped down from the tiled wall Keri and I were leaning against.

Chloe crossed her arms. "I personally think we should talk about it some more. It's an important conversation to have, after all."

Siena shrugged and turned her back to us. "Well, enjoy your banter then. I'm personally more eager to play this game than talk about it."

"Me too, actually." I stood. "I've been cooped up in this settlement for too long already."

"You're taking her side?" Chloe asked.

Keri followed my lead. "She does have the highest dungeon Survival Record."

"Second!" I bragged.

The others began following us out of the town and in the direction of the cave that would provide the Gateway to the Primatier dungeon.

"It's different for you, Noah!" Chloe shouted. "You have to survive them, so Basetier dungeons shouldn't count. Plus your parents hired a Hero rank player to protect and train you when you first began. We don't all have overprotective parents."

I guessed I really didn't calculate the advantage Datalent had given me by showing me the ropes when I first arrived.

"I'm quite happy with being the bronze medal in this argument," Keri said.

"That doesn't count either! You're a White Mage; it's your job to stay alive and support other players!"

"Maybe I should've been one of those then," I said.

"What? And paint a big target on your back? We all know that, if a party is to be wiped out, the White Mage is the first to go." David almost laughed. "You're a distance fighter, same as her, a Spellcaster with both attack and defense capabilities. You have a tank as a meat shield in front of you and a White Mage healing you from behind. You're literally in the middle of a friend zone sandwich."

Chloe hooked her arm with mine. "Who said he was in my friend zone?"

Is she trying to make Keri jealous?

Keri frowned down, and Chloe jumped back from me. "I'm only joking, Keri!"

Okay . . . I feel like I just missed something there.

With Siena_the_Blade—a maxed-out speed and borderline Hero rank player—leading us, I could see David's Stamina bar was lagging by the time we reached the foothills. On the bright side, we reached the opening of the caves leading to the Primatier dungeon in record time. Randomly generated fern bushes and palm trees were placed around the outskirts of the caves. When we arrived, Siena drew her blade and Chloe her daggers as they moved out in front. The shrubbery was the perfect place for a Chaos Engine to produce random monster encounters.

We approached cautiously, and I scanned my Key Triggers to make sure the spells I wanted were in there for shortcut use. I also made sure my Transfer Orb was at the top of my items slot just in case things started looking dire. Having the most Hit Points, David moved toward the trigger point before the bush. One of the tree's leaves rustled. It couldn't have been a Mountain Lion, but a pterodactyl-like Air Rex was still a possibility. We turned to it, and a form flew from the branches.

One of Chloe's throwing knives spun up and caught it before it could reach the sky. It fell from the air, and she took off, trying to catch the flying beast before it hit the ground and damaged the quality of her prize. It had happened so fast that I had barely seen the monster's entrance, let alone Chloe's throw.

Skidding to a stop as she caught it, Chloe pulled her knife from it and then spun, holding it up by its talons with a big grin of success on her face. "A Pheasant! Something to synth after the raid?"

After the tense situation the encounter brought on, the anti-climax of the reveal made us laugh in relief. Random encounters were just that. Sometimes it was something as weak as prey you could get a Resource Item from.

Something about Chloe's reaction to finding the monster reminded me of how excited Sue used to get when she found an ingredient on sale that she needed for a meal. Neither of us were poor. She was simply being a frugal opportunist. I never really appreciated how much it lit up everything around her until I recognized a similar expression on Chloe's face. Seeing it lent weight to the cold feeling that I might never see her again.

Come on, Noah! You're not on your own anymore, pull it together!

"Aw, and I was expecting a pre-dungeon warm up," Siena said, her Ruby Edge vanishing from her hand. Despite her confident tone, her shoulders visibly relaxed.

Chloe moved on, putting the bird in her items inventory. "Well, did that scare you off, or are you still keen for this dungeon?" she asked impatiently.

Siena moved on ahead without an answer from us, an attitude that I was getting used to. We followed her to a cave surrounded by palm trees. The warmth of the sun was replaced with cool shadows in the dark tunnel. Spindly vines hung from the ceiling, and the soil was soft enough to leave boot prints as we made our way through. The farther we walked in, the more the sound of the waves and gulls faded.

We encountered a few Rock Demons that David defeated simply by sitting on them. Seeing David use only his massive weight to defeat enemies, an idea struck me. I had heard that weight damage could be increased tenfold with gravity magic but that it also made you incredibly slow. The game creators might have overlooked how this magic affected lighter weapons. As a Spellcaster, there was nothing stopping me from learning the spell if I put my Moola into it.

I stopped and checked my stats. After this dungeon, I might have earned enough Moola and Skill Points to buy a gravity spell if I found out where to unlock it.

And if I use it with my Crystal Blades when—

"What are you staring off into space for?" Keri asked.

I shook myself from my daze.

Her expression was anxious for some reason. "You don't have to worry," she said. "I'll cast a Protection spell on you if anything dangerous shows up, and David has the Sentinel ability to guard you."

"I'm not concerned. Chaos Engines are mostly at the start of the Goblin Dungeon, right? I don't think we have much to worry about."

Siena fell back to join us and raised a ginger brow at Keri. "That's true, but for the same reason, it would be smart to be wary of the beginning. If we're really unlucky, we could be ambushed as soon as we enter."

"I go first again?" David asked.

"No way! If there's no choice but to run in blindly, then the best defense will be a good offense." Siena brushed aside her long, orange hair. "Therefore, it will be smartest for me to take the lead."

"A preemptive attack. Your favorite, right Siena?"

She gave me a stunning grin.

"We're here." Chloe's short, darkened form stopped in front of a large, glowing Gateway.

We all stood at a wide hollow in the cave. A crack in the wall let in a small line of light, making the dust glitter around the glowing green portal. Considering we'd prepared before setting off, there was nothing for us to do but select the Gateway.

"Alright, let's go!" David called.

We all selected "Goblin Dungeon" simultaneously.

David murmured, "Just to put it on record, I have a bad feeling about this."

"Shut up, David," Chloe muttered. "Your Star Wars quote is entirely inappropriate in this fantasy setting."

The portal expanded and covered our party, transporting us to the dungeon. I stayed where I was until my blurred vision gained shape. We had landed on a colossal rock bridge leaning out over an endless abyss. If this dungeon had a roof, I couldn't see it in the distant mists above us. All around it were the corpses of soldiers. David kicked the helmet of one lying on the barrier, and the skull rattled inside as it rolled away. Although only a decorative effect, the fallen soldiers certainly made for an ominous sight.

Siena stopped her charge and looked around with narrowed eyes. For some reason, no enemies were appearing.

"What's going on?" Chloe asked. "Wasn't the Chaos Engine supposed to be at the start of this dungeon?"

"So I've heard." Siena moved over the bridge. "Don't let your guard down."

The lack of dungeon monsters put me more on guard than the dark void below the bridge.

"Well, I'm glad I said it before but I have a bad feel—"

"Shut up, David!" Chloe turned to Keri. "Hurry up and cast your status effect magic. If something does appear, we'll at least be boosted for it."

"O-okay." Keri started waving around her White Rabbit Ribbon.

"I don't get it. Did the first random encounter just so happen to be nothing at all?" I suggested. "I mean, no attack at all would be just as random as a powerful demon, right?"

Siena's Ruby Edge flashed as she returned it to her items pack. "No, I don't think the Chaos Engines work that way."

Two things happened at once. The bridge began to rumble, and another glowing Gateway appeared at the other end. From it emerged, not a monster, but another party of players, at least a dozen of them charging out of it just like Siena had.

What are they doing here?

"Oh, I get it now!" David's eyes bulged.

"I think we all get it now!" Chloe said as though it were obvious.

"Well, I don't!" Keri said. "What's going on?"

Siena smiled and pointed a finger at the oncoming players. "Ha, I had no idea that random encounters included encounters with other parties coming to the dungeon!"

"You mean . . . ?" I didn't want to finish my sentence.

"Yeah," Chloe continued, her tone impatient as she raised her black daggers. "This party is the first encounter in this dungeon, and they have twice our numbers!"

Siena yelled, "I like those odds!" Her Ruby Edge flashed back into her hand, and she ran in as the other team approached.

Chapter 14

PLAYER VS. PLAYER

When Siena met the other team, one slash from her took out half of the Hit Points of one of our opponents. After a short struggle, the second swing finished him off.

I grinned and ran in after her. After all the time I'd spent grinding in easy dungeons, I wasn't going to let her have all of the fun. Passing David in his sluggish jog, I summoned a Crystal Blade and struck the first Warrior class player. The Warrior raised his own sword to parry, grinning as my blade shattered against his own. After all, my sword's durability was zero.

Behind me, the rest of the team shouted at me in surprise. Having an opponent fall for my misdirection was pretty satisfying, but having everyone be shocked by it, now that was just a thrill.

As the Warrior attempted his counterattack, I dropped to one knee and drew my hand over my shoulder for Ice

Regeneration. With a flash of Diamond Dust, another Crystal Blade appeared in my other hand, and I thrust the high strength weapon into his chest. His Hit Points went down so low from such a direct strike that all I had to do to finish him off was hit him with a Wind Blast. His body exploded from the impact.

Everyone was stunned into silence. Whether it was due to the success of my move or the looks on their faces, I couldn't help but smile. *I guess all that training I did in Lucineer wasn't a waste of time after all.*

I raised my other hand to do the gesture again, using my Ice Regeneration ability to make another Crystal Blade appear inside it.

"Whoa," Chloe murmured.

"Holy crap, Noah!" David called behind me. "You're a beast now!"

I didn't have enough time to reply as a sudden Fireball flew at me from a rival Spellcaster. I raised my Dragon Arm gauntlet to block most of the damage.

The strike was still enough to rekindle the heat of the battle with a new intensity. Jumping from his trance, David started slamming his mace into the enemy Heavy, who struck back at him. Three of Chloe's throwing knives took out the Spellcaster who had shot at me. Siena fought two enemies at once. Despite the battle being two against one, she was still doing more damage with her Ruby Edge, but I could see the pressure they were putting on her. Keri sent a healing spell.

As Siena's health regenerated, the rest of their party saw our support Spellcaster in action, and they ran at her. Maybe it was instinct from hearing Keri scream as they approached, maybe it was just the rush of the fight, but I ran in and blocked their path, using one Crystal Blade as a matador uses a cape, before reforming another blade and cutting them down. Thanks to my training, I was able to dodge most of their counterattacks, and whenever I was hit, Keri used her healing to ensure my survival. A Heavy's axe shattered one of my blades, and I dodged a sword swing from another Warrior. I spun, striking down the axe wielder before stabbing the Warrior, finishing them both off with a Fire Weave. Shards of ice and Diamond Dust rained from my attacks.

Two of the opponents were hit from behind with Chloe's throwing knives and then finished off by Siena's diving strikes. She landed behind me, sword up as though wanting to fight back-to-back, but as cool as that would have been, there were no more enemies left to kill. She groaned in disappointment. The entire party had been defeated.

Ha, we actually won!

David, who had taken the most damage out of any of us, let out a hollering victory cheer. "Woohoo!"

Laughing, Siena put an arm around my shoulders and pulled me into a headlock against her breastplate. I have to say, if the feeling of working together with a teammate was fun, then a victory of this magnitude was enough to make us all feel a little giddy.

"You little genius, Noah!" she yelled, shoving me off.

I steadied myself, and David put a hand on my shoulder, a second too late to assist me.

"You've been holding out on us," Chloe said.

"Well, this dungeon isn't over yet." I gestured to the corridor at the end of the bridge. "My attack was meant mainly for PvP, so I don't think I can play on the front lines against the monsters in here."

David pushed me, and we began to make our way down the bridge. "I don't think you understand what we just did here! That party looked like it'd done Secotier dungeons before, and we just defeated them, despite them having twice our numbers!"

Chloe snorted and crossed her arms. "It didn't look like they had very good players. Besides, we had Siena_the_Blade with us. It was hardly fair."

David brushed this off. "What I'm trying to say is there's nothing to worry about after what we just went through!"

"It's true. I've heard the only Chaos Engine in this dungeon is at the start. But it's still Primatier, so the monsters will be harder than what you're used to, Noah." Siena retook her rightful place at the head of our group, resting her sword on her shoulders. "Best stick to cover fire from now on."

I nodded as my exhilaration faded. "Alright, shall we move on then?"

Keri healed us as we made our way across the bridge to the dark corridor at its end. While we had started with a bang at the beginning of the dungeon, the rest was still pretty interesting. Although every battle environment that contained a boss was called a dungeon, this was the first one that was an actual dungeon. Dark passageways led in all directions, revealing ugly, wart-covered Goblins that attacked us with curved knives.

Always eager to go on the offensive, David and Siena cut them down as Chloe and I gave cover fire. When the Goblin's health bars hit zero, they dropped their knives and vanished.

Iron gates on the prison cells creaked open, from which more Goblins rushed out. Between ambushes, only the sound of our footfalls and the blazing torches on the wide columns filled the silence.

Without Siena here to help us, it would have been a lot more difficult. She cut enemies down so easily, and it only cost her a tiny bit of Stamina that would regenerate quickly. Even my upgraded spells that could one-shot monsters in Basetier only took half of the health of the Vampire Bats here, even less on the Goblins. With how much Mana my secondary spells used up, magic really had limitations.

I also found out why Chloe was so happy about finding the Shurikens in the Mishiji Temple, for they took down the bats just as quickly as Siena. The only downside was their retrieval time. She had to wait in the same spot for them to fly back to her. She had bragged about her speed earlier in the day, and it seemed she was glad for the opportunity to show it off because she didn't say a word about us not waiting for her.

Around my friends and allies, I could really let go of my fear and just have fun. I would even go so far as to say that the fear was a part of what made it fun, like the times when I went to see a horror film with Sue.

After several waves of Goblins, we arrived at the final room, and holy crap, what a room. Blazing torches shone up on the walls, illuminating large chests and keys for the cells hanging on large hooks. At the back of the hall was a large chair that the boss sat on as though it were a throne. The boss was a kind of Goblin, but five times the size of the previous ones. He wore a blue uniform that his belly bulged out from, and as we approached, he grabbed for the truncheon hanging by his side.

— The Warden —

This guy definitely wins the award for ugliest boss. I stayed back, waiting to see how tough this guy was going to be before I got too close. I still had my Transfer Orb ready to go, but after how well the dungeon had been going, I really didn't want to have to use it.

"I'm going to have me that whacking stick," David said, rubbing his gauntleted hands.

The Warden crouched, slapping his belly in an invitation to attack. David took the invitation, taking the brunt of the Warden's first swing. Thanks to his armor, it did less damage than it would have to any of us. However, as Chloe and I began tossing Shurikens and spells at him, more Goblin prison guards proceeded to emerge from the tunnels.

"I'll handle them," Siena said, running toward the entrance to hold them back at the doorway

David continued to attack the Warden head on, taking small chunks of Hit Points with each blow, but it was looking like even Keri's support wouldn't keep him alive long enough to win the fight. I then realized that the protective stats that Keri had given us at the start of the dungeon had worn off.

"David, fall back!" I yelled.

He turned and just barely managed to dodge a swing from the truncheon that would have killed him.

"Keri, your spells have worn off!"

"Sorry!" Keri went about casting her supportive magic, which left her with barely enough Mana to cast a healing spell.

I still had enough Hit Points left that I could take the Warden's attention away from David's retreat for a time. His blows against David had been powerful, but not enough to kill me as long as I moved quickly.

"Cover me!" I called to Chloe.

"What?"

I ran around the giant Goblin, forming my Crystal Blades and then stabbing them into him. The skin around his hide was so thick that the blades broke off with only one swing, but the damage done was still significant. His backside looked like an icy hedgehog. I danced long enough around the Warden's back that Keri's Mana could regenerate. She quickly healed David's low Hit Points, and he stepped forward to rejoin the fight.

As Siena kept the other Goblins at bay, we worked together to finish off the boss, dodging his swings as he desperately tried to defend himself. It was a fruitless effort. The Warden soon dropped to his knees, the floor rumbling as he fell heavily onto the stone. Siena almost looked disappointed as the giant body began to melt into a bubbling pool of sludge. I guessed she hadn't expected us to finish off the boss before she'd gotten rid of the Goblin minions, but I'd been able to hold my own in this fight. I was relieved my friends weren't going to have to worry about me in Primatier dungeons anymore. The game was a lot more fun when I didn't have to cower behind everyone else.

The girls jumped back as the Goblin goo spread out over the floor.

"Ew, it even smells bad," Siena said, grabbing her nose.

It really did smell awful, like mayonnaise that had gone bad in the sun.

"Well, you are the one who chose this dungeon." I turned to David. "Go check the chests in those indents, and I bet you'll find a version of that truncheon."

"Way ahead of you," David said, kicking open the lid of one. "Oh yeah, there we go!"

He pulled out a club similar to the Warden's truncheon and seemed thrilled with its stats. The other chest contained an armored dress for a female Warrior. Probably why Siena had wanted to do this dungeon in the first place.

"Who would have expected to find such a nice little dress in a place like this?" she said as she picked it up.

It made sense considering she was the only Warrior in our party.

"Aren't Goblins known for kidnapping women?" David asked. "You know, regular monster stuff?"

Keri looked around. "If that's her dress, where's the woman?"

"What happened to the girls in those tales?" Chloe continued with an evil grin. "Probably eaten."

"No!" Keri gasped.

Siena made the dress vanish into her items. "If that's the case, she won't need it."

As I'd made habit of after every dungeon, I searched the area. For the first time since the tutorial, an arrow appeared in my vision. I turned in the direction it was pointing. To one side of the Warden's office was a desk, and on the desk was a torn piece of notepaper with a mindless scrawl on it. It was an item. I touched it, and it automatically went into my inventory.

— Acquired Torn Note Piece! —

My eyebrows knitted together. *That's strange.*

For some reason, no new option appeared when I brought it up in my menu, so I put the item away and turned back to everyone. I felt like I could trust all of the people in my party, so I pulled out the Transfer Orb Brock had given me, readying it to return to town.

David's eyes bulged. "How did you get one of those?"

"It was a gift."

Siena's brow furrowed, as though suspicious someone would have given one away. "From who?"

"My friend, Brock."

"Ah, him," Siena said as though it made so much sense that it annoyed her.

Chloe turned on me. "You know both Brockodile and Siena_the_Blade, you were trained by Datalent, *and* you've figured out a weapon-ability tactic that would allow you to survive in a Secotier dungeon this early on?"

"Technically," David put a finger up, "I knew Brock first."

"Shut up, David!"

I shrugged, gesturing to the orb. "You want to use this to go back or not?"

"Fine," she said, moving in with Keri and David.

"I'm staying here for a while," Siena said. "Want to test out this new getup. I'll see you later, and if you see Data again, tell him he still owes me."

I wanted to call her out on what sounded like an obvious lie, but she ran off before I could.

Without exchanging another word, they all touched the glowing orb, and as the Key Trigger showed up, we teleported back to the tropical city of Yarburn.

"I'm going AFB," Chloe said as soon as we arrived.

"I'll talk to you later," Keri said.

"You're not . . . ? " She sighed, looking suddenly annoyed. "Whatever."

She vanished without going to the Gateway. I guessed

that she felt her DSD wearing off and wanted to wake up.

Keri gave me a charming smile. Maybe even she needed time away from her friend.

"So, what do you want to do?" I asked.

David shrugged his massive shoulders. "I wouldn't mind checking out the rankings."

Keri didn't look like she cared.

We moved down the street, taking in the tropical town. The rankings were on the way to the Synth Square in this town. I had earned just enough Skill Points to get the gravity spell, and I had heard you could get a hint on where to gain access to it if you asked the NPCs there.

As we made our way to the street with the new Wanted Boards, David rushed back to us with a wide smile on his face.

"Noah, you're not going to believe this!"

He dragged me to the Wanted Board and pointed out a poster on the Primatier line. I was surprised to see my own face looking back at me.

"That's you, man!" David yelled.

I then remembered what Siena had told me about the time conversion when going from Basetier to Primatier. After how many consecutive days I had been living in Basetier for, it was only logical that, after this conversion and the dungeon we had just finished, I would've had enough time to have achieved the rank.

I then recalled Brock telling me that getting a Wanted rank would be like kicking a beehive for me.

I'm now officially a wanted man.

Chapter 15

TOO MANY COINCIDENCES

Waves crashed against the sand as Keri and I walked down the Yarburn beach. She'd insisted that she wanted to spend more time with me so I wouldn't be alone in here, and I didn't have the heart to tell her I was used to it by now. That would've been a little too depressing, even for me.

The sound of the rolling tide followed us along the shore, just like our footprints. As we walked, our trails vanished into the distance.

The beach had the orange sky of dusk. Widows' Forest was in a nighttime setting, Galrinth was set during daylight, and Lucineer was so snowy that it barely mattered. It made me curious about how the day/night cycles might look if one could observe all of Basetier from on high.

"I think I was wrong when I said I like extroverts," Keri said, hands held behind her. "I really like people who surprise me. It's hard to imagine that you're already Wanted, even though you've only been playing for two weeks."

Has it really been that long?

I figured this was a test to see how humble I was. "I have very little else that I can do. I still haven't gotten what I need to truly make my strategy effective yet, though."

I was preparing a lie to keep my plan a secret, but it turned out she was more perceptive than I had thought.

"You're going to try to get the gravity spell, aren't you?"

I gave her a look.

She smiled shyly and linked arms with me. "Come on, Noah, I'm a Spellcaster as well, and I've seen the stats of your Crystal Blades. The reason they have no durability is because they have very little weight to them. With the gravity spell your weapon's weight only increases a little, but everyone else's would become unmanageable. Am I right?"

Busted.

I sighed. "You just know everything, don't you?"

"I only know magic—support magic mostly—and if you think about it, that's exactly what gravity is." She sighed. "There's only one problem with your strategy."

I grinned. She was begging to show off her own knowledge. "Oh yeah?"

"Originally, the gravity spell was learned by defeating certain bosses, but now it can only be accessed through defeating a Spellcaster who possesses it. That's why it's unlikely for White Mages like me to be able to learn it." She ran a finger up my arm. "You might have a chance, if you get to the Secotier dungeons, that is."

"I assume that's where those who want to learn the spell go to gain access to it?" I said. "Which means that, to complete my strategy, I'll have to defeat a Spellcaster there?"

Keri nodded. "I can help you once we go through all the Primatier dungeons. There's still a lot to do there." She looked up at me as we walked, eyes sparkling.

The sky began to change again. We were walking out of the sunset-covered region of the beach into the night area of the connecting peninsula, which eventually led to the tail end of Widows' Forest. The darkness felt like a natural accompaniment to our walk.

I turned to walk back into the more well-lit area of the map, but Keri grabbed me by the sleeve of my robe and pulled me further into the darkness. She seemed to be leading me somewhere we could not be seen by others. When we stopped, she grabbed me by my arms, and I thought she was going to kiss me. I froze, unwilling to lean in but not ready to pull away from her just yet.

"Wait," she said. Pulling away from me, she turned to face a hooded figure in the darkness. "Who are you?"

The tall, robed avatar took out a weapon, the green blade glowing in the darkness. It was Bitcon.

Sudden panic arose in me. "Keri, Protection spell, now!"

As soon as this left my lips, the assailant ran at me. Crystal Blades flashed from Diamond Dust into my hands. I raised one, and it was smashed into shards against the rare weapon. But I was prepared for this result. Another blade formed in my hands, and I struck again. My own force against his weapon broke the blade, and as another formed to deflect his next attack, Keri's spell began to take effect, a protective bubble forming around me. I doubted that Protection would do much against the Jade Edge, but I had to try.

I pushed him back with a Wind Blast and tried to use Ice Wall to create a barrier between us, but Bitcon just blasted through it with a Fireball. I couldn't understand why he was attacking me on Basetier where there was nothing he could gain from it, not even my Primatier Wanted rank.

"What do you need?" Keri asked frantically.

"Speed!" I yelled back, and she started casting the spell.

Bitcon spun and charged her way. I chased after him, but I was too late. Keri screamed, struck down in two quick slashes. It was over so quickly. I couldn't have done anything to help her.

A sudden light covered me, and I could feel the speed of Keri's final spell come over me like I had just taken a load of caffeine all at once. I ran at Bitcon, using my advantage while it lasted. I struck at him, and he blocked. One at a time, my blades shattered against his, each one a distraction for the attack that came after, but he was just too quick. I finally managed to get a slash in and then another.

Bitcon cut the next two away with wide sweeping strikes, but I persisted, striking and evading with all of my Stamina as my blades continued to shatter. His strategy seemed to involve breaking my blades to hit me. My ability wasn't free, and my Mana continued to shrink with each blade I regenerated. But unfortunately for him, this was also a part of my own strategy. I wasn't landing many strikes and yet his health was still going down.

I knew my Crystal Blades did a lot of damage. Aside from the Warden, I'd only used them on low level monsters before. Not on someone like him. Apparently, they worked on tough players too.

Bitcon flipped back from one of my attacks, and this gave me enough time to compare our Hit Points. I was shocked to see that I was winning, by a lot. I couldn't help but wonder how someone as skilled as Data hadn't managed to land a single blow on this guy, yet his health was dropping against me like he was poisoned by Arachnid venom.

He didn't charge forward again. He simply stared at me and raised his arms out to his sides.

Two smaller blades suddenly spun past me towards Bitcon, and I heard Chloe call, "Noah!" as she ran up behind me.

Bitcon was still standing with his arms spread, unmoving despite Chloe's black knives having taken away a good portion of his dwindling health.

Does he want me to finish him off?

"Who are you?"

Bitcon didn't respond. He just curled his fingers, beckoning me to attack. I decided to oblige him before he could kill Chloe like he had Keri. I ran in, stabbing my Crystal Blade through him to take out his last Hit Points. Just before he died, I looked up under his hood and saw those horn-like bumps again. This time I also saw his grinning mouth. He vanished in a bright flash, leaving me with the feeling that I had seen that grin somewhere before, but I couldn't quite place where.

Then two windows appeared before me. The first one showed the usual blank avatar. It raised its arm in the air before lowering it down in front of itself as a warping animation covered the space in front of it.

— Ability to learn Gravity Pull unlocked! —

Bitcon must have known the gravity spell.

The next window had a glowing image of a fading

piece of paper.

— Acquired Torn Note Piece! —

"You're kidding!"

Chloe ran to me in concern. "What is it?"

It didn't make any sense. In Basetier, you couldn't take any of your opponent's items after beating them. This meant that Bitcon had dropped the note. But why?

Before, when I had received the Torn Note Piece from the Goblin Dungeon, I couldn't read it. This time when I pulled up the menu to see what the item was for, the option "Read" appeared in my Key Triggers. I decided to leave these suspicions for another time. After Chloe had gone out of her way to save me, she more than deserved some of my attention.

"You beat him . . . a Color Blade!" she exclaimed.

"You didn't see it all," I denied. "Keri helped . . . but thank you."

"With support, sure! Color Blades usually only play on Seco- and Tertiatier! You defeated him one-on-one after she was killed!"

I shook my head and got out of my menu. "I don't know. Something tells me he wanted to be defeated. After all, on Basetier he wouldn't lose any items."

Chloe kicked my legs out from under me so I was forced to look up at her fierce glare. "That's not what I'm talking about! You didn't use your Transfer Orb to get away. You obviously don't care about the consequences of losing a fight!"

I burned with indignation. "I forgot, okay?" I pulled her down to her knees to face me. "Can't you see I'm terrified of losing and becoming comatose? Don't you think that maybe fear was the reason I acted instinctively to defend myself? Unlike all of you, I actually want to return to reality!"

"Where all your friends are leaving you for this game?" she asked.

I realized she was right. This was exactly what I had been complaining about to Sue before the crash.

"David told me. You talk about returning to reality, but what do you even have there?"

"Not Sue . . ." This argument with Chloe reminded me of the ones I used to have with her.

"What?" Chloe looked less aggressive and more attentive now.

I sighed. "The car accident that got me stuck in here put my girlfriend in critical condition. The doctors have tried to use the Dream Engine to get her in here like me, but so far, it's been unsuccessful. There's a high likelihood that she'll be dead by the time I finally wake up."

"Seems to me that what you need is another reason to want to stick around." She put her hands on her hips, her tone lowering. "Well, if that's the case . . ."

With our faces so close, she only had to lean in a little to kiss me on the lips.

I was so shocked that I almost let out a hysterical laugh, but I managed to hold it in.

Before I could say anything in reaction, she stood and turned. "Don't die. You owe me now, you know?"

I couldn't get a word in before she vanished into the night. All I could do was shake my head and wonder what was going on in that girl's head.

Still kneeling there by myself, I tried to find a way to

distract my nerves from the adrenaline that was pumping through my mind. I pulled up my menu and focused on the two Torn Note Pieces. The Key Trigger option to read them popped up again. I selected it, and a note in rough script appeared in my vision.

> *It's dark and I don't know where I am. All I recall is our car being hit by that truck on the highway. Afterward, I found myself in this room. I haven't eaten or drunk anything for a week now, and yet I don't feel hungry or thirsty. I hear people talking outside and the rumbling of earth. They say that it's called Tertiatier or Rubik's something, but I've never heard of such a place.*

The note read almost like a letter.

> *I've been experiencing illusions. I'm not sure, but when I wrote my last note, it vanished from the room. Although now I wouldn't be surprised if even that paper hadn't been real at all. Every so often, I hear the howling of wind and feel cold air rush into this place. I tried to find an exit, but I haven't seen any of the faces of my captors, although I have heard them. They talk about how cold and how high up we are. The entrance must be somewhere in the mountains. Will he save me from this place, or did the crash kill him too?*

Sue.

It was unlikely, but the letter sounded like her. The length of time she'd been trapped and the mention of the car crash all hinted at it being Sue.

But how? Did she manage to connect to the Dream Engine?

It sounded like she was being kept in a Tertiatier dungeon against her will.

I didn't hesitate to send my mother the message: "I need to talk."

My mother's tired face appeared on my contact's video feed a moment later.

"What is it, dear?" she asked attentively.

"Has Sue managed to connect to the Dream Engine yet?"

My mother's brow furrowed. "We're not sure. The connection light is on, but . . . there's no other sign that she's responding to the drugs. Because of the helmet, we can't check brain activity using an MRI . . . but the connection light is shining, so . . ."

I grinned. "I see. Thank you."

"Are you alright?" she asked, her voice suddenly anxious. "You sound different."

That's hope you're hearing.

"I'm fine. I'll talk to you later."

I disconnected the call before she could reply.

Sue was in the Dream State. She had to be.

Chapter 16
THE ONJIRA PLAINS

The Synth Square of Yarburn was similar to the others I'd seen. However, Yarburn's paths were bridges over a massive pool of clear water. I made my way to the spell store and bought the gravity spell I had just gained access to. After I had performed the light ceremony that endowed me with the spell, I knew it was time to contact Data. If I was going to find Sue, I would need his help.

We met at one of the Synth Square's outer benches, and he sat opposite to me.

"I'm surprised you came."

"Your parents paid Wona to add an extra week to the contract for me to check up on you now and then. They're really worried about you."

I wish you told me that when I messaged you. I'd been planning how to convince him to help me.

"You know, you're lucky you had Siena here to look after

you," he said. "I heard you did a Primatier dungeon. That was silly of you."

My plan wouldn't work if he was trying to keep me out of the upper levels. "Weren't you the one who said that I shouldn't limit myself in-game if I wanted to have fun?"

He shrugged. "You should have contacted me is all I'm saying."

"Well, you should be glad I waited for you before going into the Tertiatier dungeon. Would you happen to know which of the Gateways is at the top of a mountain or somewhere high up and cold?"

Data raised his hands. "Hold your horses, Noah! What are you, suicidal? You are in no way ready for a Tertiatier dungeon!"

I didn't entirely disagree, but I had no choice. Now that I knew Sue was inside the game, I had hope for the first time since the accident. She might actually live through this. But she didn't have Data looking out for her, and she was trapped inside a Tertiatier dungeon. If she was ever going to wake up again, she would need to get out of there alive.

"I'll admit, I have a lot more to lose than you," I said, "but you'd be surprised how much I've improved since you've been away."

"Tsh, not nearly enough! Even I find the Tertiatier dungeons difficult!"

I shook my head. "All the more reason to get prepared well in advance. Anyway, take a look at this."

I gave him the Torn Note Piece items to have a look at. He read it in his window, which looked odd, as it was invisible to me. I tried not to fidget while I waited.

When he was done, he stroked his chin in thought.

"Someone must have done some digging on you when they saw you on the Wanted Boards."

"What do you mean?"

He gave me back the note items and pointed to my menu. From the visible and invisible labels, I had assumed that players could only see another's Hit Points, Mana, and Stamina bars, but seeing another player's items menu must have been something you could gain access to as a Hero rank player.

"It reads like bait to me, written by someone who probably wants to lure you to a Tertiatier dungeon where they can kill you and take all of your stuff."

The only rare item I had was the Transfer Orb Brock had given me, but only those who had come with me to Goblin Dungeon knew about it. I doubted any of them would be trying to lure me into a trap.

Bitcon had dropped the note. Did that mean he was the one holding Sue hostage? If so, Data's theory about it being a trap was probably right. But it didn't change anything. *The note is too specific.* I couldn't leave Sue trapped there.

"I still want to check it out."

"Why?"

I didn't have an answer that would convince him. He had no reason to care about Sue.

His chin stroke became a scratch. "Although a trap doesn't work half as well without the surprise."

I nodded. "And, if I spring it on my terms, I might be able to turn the tables on whoever set it. Besides, if it's a Tertiatier dungeon, you might be able to get Bitcon's Color Blade off him . . . so how about it?"

"Tsh, your parents may have paid me a lot, but still not

enough to put my own Color Blade on the line."

"Then don't use it! You can't have it stolen unless its equipped, right? Surely, you're good enough to survive this raid without it?"

He thought for a while longer. "On one condition. If we're going to be fighting this guy in a Tertiatier dungeon, you're going to have to get a lot stronger."

"You want me to max my stats in Primatier first? Fine."

"With how good you've apparently become, it should only take a week. If you spend a couple of days doing some of the Prima- and Secotier dungeons, I will agree to come with you on this fool's errand. Deal?" He put his hand out.

It made sense that he wanted me to hold off for a week. That's how long his contract with my parents lasted. But I couldn't argue with a few days. I had been planning to spend a few days maxing out my new abilities in Primatier before doing this dungeon anyway. I was no help to Sue unless I could survive long enough to get to her.

I knocked his hand away. "Okay, but you better be fully on board when we do go."

"Don't misunderstand me. I want to confront this thing just as much as you do." He shrugged. "Besides, even with your skill, I doubt you would make it to the Gateway. The monsters around the Tertiatier dungeons are the hardest monsters in Basetier."

They're still Basetier monsters. But I didn't say anything. I didn't want him to change his mind. Instead, I started making my way to the Gateway. Data was forced to catch up with me.

"You know more about gear than anyone I've talked to so far," I said. "What are some of the best dungeons to get

Resource Items to synth?"

"I'm your tailor now?" he said in that sarcastic tone of his. "You'll need new robes and a Cursed Druid Staff. The best robes for your needs would come from the Druids' Keep dungeon. You'll want to fight Merlin Owls to get Night Down. As for the staff, we can get Ironwood from the Onjira Rainforest." Data sighed. "We'll have to bathe it in the Cursed Pool while we're at the Keep as well."

Onjira Plains was where Data had gotten his own armor. It sounded good enough to me.

The list of areas appeared in my menu as we reached the Gateway.

"Well, if we need to dip the Ironwood in the waters of the Druids' Keep, we might as well head to Onjira first."

"You seem eager to get to an extreme environment." Data opened his window. "You'll regret being so hasty."

"I don't want to waste time. If you say that this is the fastest way, then we might as well get it over with. Besides . . ." I sneered at Data. "You're the one who doesn't seem to want to return there. I want to see what all the fuss is about. Time to earn what my parents are paying you."

I selected the menu option for Onjira. As soon as we arrived, I felt the heat and the dry, dusty wind in my face. I groaned. Through the sandstorm, I could see what might have been a desert if the sand hadn't been blown off most of the bushes and hardpan. It was the flattest place I'd seen in the Dream State so far, which would have given us a lot of prior warning for any attacking monsters, if it weren't for the harsh wind and distant heat waves hampering our vision. The dry trees mushroomed above the minor scrub. It looked like the Kalahari Desert, and I could only imagine the monsters here were similar in nature as well.

Data grinned, squinting into the wind. "Tsh, you were saying?"

"Didn't you say that there's a rainforest out here?"

"Yeah, but it's a good distance away, so let's get going. I learned firsthand how annoying it is not to have a Gateway nearby," Data said. "I tried to get my superiors to ask the game designers to make one closer, but they only said they would take it under consideration."

I wished I could use my Transfer Orb to get us past the oppressive heat, but since I'd never been there before, we would have to take the long way.

Data equipped a pair of spectacles and began to walk. After seeing Brock's goggles in Lucineer, I had caved and bought a pair of my own for seeing through the blizzards. It seemed Lucineer wasn't the only place they could come in handy. I equipped mine as well.

The first monster we ran into was a Sand Leopard. It leaped down from one of the squat trees. The monster resembled the curve-fanged Mountain Lion we fought outside the Penance Mines, but its color was a lighter hue. With a flash, Data drew out his fixed dual-swords, and I managed to get in a Fireball before Data cut it in two. It dropped to the sand, and we moved on.

The next was a Diving Bird with black feathers and an elongated beak. It swooped down from the sky to attack us, and I destroyed it with a single blast of lightning. Unlike the rest of my beginner spells, Lightning Strike was one I never had much reason to use, but fighting flying monsters seemed reason enough. The large bird vanished before hitting the sand. We collected the Black Feather it dropped and moved on. I was ready to be out of the desert and in the cool shade of the rainforest.

Next, we ran into the Rhino that Data had gotten Resource Items from for his armor. It appeared from behind a thorn bush, and I could see from the wide ridges and thick skin exactly how this monster could have provided such armor.

"Watch its charges!" Data said. "Getting hit by its horn can do some serious damage."

We were forced to avoid it, Data's dual swords barely doing any damage to its thick skin.

After a few close calls and a lot of useless lightning magic, I found that Earth Mold was the most effective spell against it. The monster would stun itself when it broke through the wall of dirt, leaving a few seconds for Data to stab it directly in its eyes and belly. After a couple of these barrages, the Rhino fell to its knees, tucked its head, and vanished with a flash.

As we continued, we ran into several more Rhinos and Diving Birds. The Birds we got through quickly, but each Rhino took us several minutes to get through their ridiculously high defense.

Of the six we killed, we only received two Rhino Hides.

"How many Rhino Hides did you have to earn to get your gear?" I asked. "And how many Rhinos did you have to beat to get them?"

"About fifty Hides all up. I lost count of the number of Rhinos I had to kill."

"What? But why? The armor looks like it would barely need two of them!"

Data sighed. "I know, I thought the same. It's

ridiculous because the Rhino Hides are refined ten to one for Rhino Leathers."

I cringed at the idea of spending hours farming such a Resource Item in this hot place. The game designers must have been sadists. "Jeez, and I thought the grind in Lucineer was bad."

"Don't sell yourself short," Data said. "There are three places in Basetier considered extreme environments and Lucineer is one of them."

"Of the two, I think I prefer training in Lucineer."

We moved on, the Onjira Rainforest rising out of the rippling heat wave on the horizon. I was already anticipating the cool shade that the trees would bring.

"Where's the third place?" I asked.

Data grinned. "You'll see soon enough. Let's just say that every game should have a good lava level, and if you think this place is hot, then you don't know what you're in for."

It was hard to imagine, but I would cross that bridge when I came to it. For now, I just needed to get some Ironwood.

When we reached the lush rainforest, I could see right away why these trees were used for weapons. They were thick, dark, and hard to the touch.

"How do we cut them down?"

Data stopped, looking around the rainforest for other players before equipping his Sapphire Edge. "Any other weapon would break against them, and I don't want you to waste your Moola for this." He sighed. "I guess it's my job to cut down some of these. What I need you to do is circle the surrounding area and fight any monsters nearby that might try to sneak up on me. Got it?"

"Should I come back in twenty minutes?"

Data took a swing at a tree he had picked out. "Tsh, more like an hour. That should be long enough to train in the surrounding area."

I guess it's better than just waiting around for him to finish. It seemed a bit pointless, protecting a guy with a Color Blade, but I figured I might as well go and explore.

"Alright, I'll see you in an hour."

The Onjira Rainforest was infinitely larger than the one in Yarburn. Hills led down to streams and rivers and then rose again, thick with jungle. The trees spread around me as I combed the area for monsters. Uphill and then down in the direction of another river, I came across a few Diving Birds, blowing them out of the sky with lightning like before. Eventually, the hour was almost up, and I began to make my way back to where I had left Data.

Without warning, a Sand Leopard jumped down on top of me, letting out a low growl as its claws caught on my buckler. I equipped a Crystal Blade as its fangs sank into my shoulder, letting the cat take some of my Hit Points in order to bury my sword into its rib cage. It collapsed on top of me before vanishing.

Checking my health bar, I laughed in relief upon seeing how little damage I had taken. *I guess we are still in Basetier. I'm strong enough now that nothing here should be able to kill me that easily.*

When I finally returned, I could see that Data had cut down a large tree that was now glowing, ready to be collected.

He smiled as he noticed the sheen on my forehead. "You look hot."

"You don't."

"My time in Onjira built up my hot temperature

tolerance," he said. "Being here will do the same for you."

"What do you mean?"

Data almost laughed. "I'm surprised that you didn't notice during your time in Lucineer. Bring up your menu and check your stats, it should be above the weight of your gear."

I pulled up my menu and saw that there was an incredibly high number next to the symbol that looked like a snowflake.

"It's one of my highest stats. What does it mean?"

"You must have noticed your comfort level there increasing. It would also have increased your defense against ice attacks."

I felt a little stupid for not noticing earlier. This was most likely the reason why I had improved exponentially during my time in Lucineer. I'd thought I was just getting really good at the game.

"The same goes for my time in Onjira. As you can see, I've built up enough heat tolerance to not even sweat now. Just remember that raising your tolerance for one type of temperature will lower your tolerance for the other."

I'd first thought that Data had survived Bitcon's Kamikaze blast because he was Hero rank. Now I was beginning to think it was because of his built-up defense to fire magic.

"Well, it's good to know I would have survived most ice attacks."

"Tsh, what kind of idiot trained you?"

I cocked an eyebrow at his knowing grin, and couldn't help but laugh.

"So, we've got some Ironwood." I bent down to put it into my inventory. "Now we can go to the Druids' Keep, right?"

Data nodded and turned in the direction of the hills

farther inside the forest. "The Druids' Keep is a Secotier dungeon, which we can access here. The only reason you'll be able to access it is because, together, our accumulated Skill Points should be enough. Do you see what I'm saying?"

"It's a dungeon with a high difficulty level."

"Right. Since it's been recently updated, I'm almost tempted to call Siena to help us out on this one." He began to move in swift strides through the forest, stroking his chin in his characteristic thinking expression. I could almost see a loading bar filling up on his forehead. "Would any of your friends be willing to join us?"

I thought about who I should ask. "A few, David, Chloe, Keri, Bro—"

"Not Brock!"

"Right, you two don't see eye to eye. It's hard to imagine anyone having a grudge against him. He's a pretty chill guy."

"'One may smile, and smile, and be a villain,'" Data said.

"Shakespeare?"

He smirked. "Tsh, good guess."

It wasn't a guess. I'd studied Hamlet in freshman year. But sometimes it was better to let people assume you were an idiot.

At the bottom of the hill, we ran into a river that led out of the forest. I spotted the sprawling Onjira Village in the distance. The river we were following cut through the entire settlement, the curving domes atop a few of the taller buildings giving it an Arabian look. We soon arrived at the Gateway outside the village. For an extreme environment, the place sure was crowded.

Grinding for Rhino Hides perhaps?

We had decided to get Siena_the_Blade involved, as she

was someone I knew Data was comfortable playing with. While we waited for her, I noticed that a lot more of the players in this part of Basetier were riding on mounts. From what Data had told me, Onjira dungeons were a better place to train for higher-level players.

I recognized one of the Spellcaster avatars that landed nearer to us on his Griffin, remembering his sharp features from the Wanted Boards. Strangely, he was staring straight at me with cold eyes. It wasn't until another player came to his side that he looked away. He must have recognized me from my own Wanted poster. Luckily, he left me alone in Basetier.

"See that elf-looking tank over there?" Data pointed to a Heavy who flew an obnoxiously massive, black serpent down to meet with the two I had been watching. "That's Sirswift, the guy I told you about with the highest Tertiatier Survival Record."

So, that's the best player in the Dream State. He doesn't look like much.

Sirswift leaped off his mount. His avatar wasn't as big as David's, but he carried a massive sword, so big it looked ridiculous on him. His face had been altered to look like a Tolkien-style elf, and golden spirals adorned his black armor.

"Introduce me to him," I said, hoping to call out Data's relationship with him as an empty boasting.

"Alright." Data shrugged and then called, "Hey, Swifty!"

Sirswift's pointed ears twitched in our direction, and he said something to his teammates. He then turned and walked over to us.

"Data, I'm getting ready for a dungeon," he snapped. "What do you want?"

"I'm sure you can spare a little time to talk to an old friend."

"I have very little free time these . . ." He trailed off as his cold eyes shifted to me. "He's the one . . . the one who achieved a Wanted rank in Primatier during his first dungeon."

Data inclined his head. "That's him."

I suddenly felt embarrassed that I had become the center of attention. "You could say I found a brand new way of playing the game."

Sirswift smirked. "I wouldn't say stacking time in Basetier is a new idea. You just happen to be in a situation where you have no choice."

My eyebrows knitted together. "Wait, how did you know that?"

"Hurry up and get to Tertiatier." He turned away from us. "Then we'll see if you have any real skill."

He moved back to his friends, the crowd parting for him until he came to his massive mount.

"Not a very social fellow, is he?" Data said, cocking an eyebrow.

I nodded. "He talks like an elitist."

"Tsh, that's because he is one." Data stuck out his bottom lip. "But I guess you need that kind of attitude if you want to get as good as he is."

The three Wanted players took off for whichever crazy hard dungeon they were doing next. Five minutes later, Siena arrived. She appeared with a flash beside us, wearing the Warrior garment she had acquired in the Goblin Dungeon, a tightly linked chainmail dress that went down to her knees.

She ruffled my hair. "You've decided to take a shot at the big leagues, huh?"

I shrugged. "I suppose so. It won't really be the big leagues until I reach Tertiatier, right?"

Siena rolled her eyes. "Don't get too big for your britches, Noah. We'll get there eventually."

"Well, when I'm ready, I'll be sure to tell you."

If there was one player who I'd want to bring along with me to a higher tier dungeon, it would be Siena.

Chapter 17

THE DRUIDS' KEEP

As we exited the Gateway atop a high staircase in the Onjira Hills, I was in awe of the fortress's size. The Keep was a tall, wide tower with an outer staircase spiraling up its circumference to its ruined peak. Rumbling clouds crept in over the distant hills and blocked some of the sunlight, bathing the tower in melancholic shadows. The whole place looked like an ancient ruin.

"Ha, this place really did get an update since we last came here," Siena said.

We moved across the hill path toward the massive door to the Keep.

"I remember the story behind this place; it's linked to a Tertiatier castle dungeon in Lucineer and another north of the Storm Wall," Data said. "The Druids here were corrupted when a Dark Warrior visited them. I've heard the tale has progressed to the point that the Druids have gone mad, and the Dark Warrior now sits at its top in front of the Cursed Pool."

"The place we need to get to." I smirked. "Maybe I should

have gotten in contact with the others, after all."

Data pulled open the rusted doors. "Tsh, too late now. Let's get this over with."

The doors creaked loudly as they swung open to reveal a massive open hall with the beginnings of a spiral staircase up on a high mezzanine. There was only one thing in the hall, one small person in a dusty cloak, pacing back and forward.

"Our first insane Druid?" Siena asked.

"Noah, fire a spell his way and see how he reacts," Data said.

I nodded and launched an ice spell at the mad Druid. My Ice Wall spell had been upgraded to Ice Coffin during my training in the Lucineer Mountains. After a few seconds of the spell draining my Mana, the mumbling man was encased in a block of ice.

"Well, that was easy enough," Siena said in surprise.

There was an audible crack from the ice, followed by an explosion that almost filled the entire hall. The Druid stood with arms raised as the flames spun around him.

"He took it well," Data said with his usual dry sarcasm. "If you can blow that fire away from me, I'll be able to take him out."

"I have just the spell."

I used Wind Blast to blow the fire away from Data's area of the room. Data went to move in but was overtaken by Siena, who ran in and slashed at the Druid. Data only managed to get in a single attack before the old Druid vanished with a flutter of old, black feathers. Night Down.

I picked a few of them up. Obviously, Merlin Owls weren't the only monsters that dropped them, which made a new robe a little easier to achieve.

Siena looked around. Before the fight, the floor had been covered in dust, but the wind from my spell had cleared it away to reveal the bright patterns on the floor. She rushed up to the balcony that led to the spiral staircase outside.

My footsteps echoed loudly as I followed her. "I can't figure out if she wants to lead the way or just can't stay still for long."

"Whatever she needs, this game must be a good outlet for it." Data moved up the stairs after her. "Just look at this place. You should have seen the Keep before the Dark Warrior turned up. Wona's designers have been busy."

I rolled my eyes. "We can't do a single dungeon without you trying to sell this game, even though we're already playing it."

"Ha, is that really how I sound?" Data asked with humor in his tone. "It's hard to break the habit of a salesman, but you are lucky to be stuck in this of all games."

Looking around the huge insides of the Keep, I couldn't help but agree with him, especially when I thought about the crappy MMO games I'd played in the past. The artificial sunlight made the motes of dust glitter in the openings leading to the spiral staircase. The outer banister led up to a window, revealing a beautiful view of the green countryside that spanned further with every floor. I was so caught up in it that I barely had any time to worry about other things. The escapism was as addictive as any drug, and ironically, the source of this escapism came from a drug.

When we reached the second floor, after a ridiculous number of stairs, we entered into another massive hall. Another Druid roamed the balcony. We moved in from the stairwell as a sudden whirlwind cleared the dust from the massive murals. The robed Druid was lifted up from the mezzanine and flipped once in the air before landing on the floor before us.

"Wind this time. I have a feeling these floors are going to have a Druid for each type of spell." Siena shrugged. "Oh well, I feel better killing these crazy guys than having to kill those cute little owls the Spellcasters used to farm here."

I almost laughed. "I have just the thing for this."

I rose my arm and lowered it again, casting Gravity Pull on Data and Siena. I could see their surprise as their weight increased four-fold. This may have slowed them down, but as the second Druid used his wind to blow them back, it barely managed to lift them in their heavy armor.

And other games thought their elemental dichotomy was done well.

Data began to move into the gust, slowly raising his sword as the dust and air rushed at him. He put on his goggles to see where he should strike, but unlike his leathers, Siena's chain mail was too heavy for her to assist him this time. He didn't need it. The gravitational pull on his weapon gave his downward cut even more strength than the Sapphire Edge usually packed. The Druid vanished in a puff of dust.

Data shook himself, and dust poured out of every nook and cranny of his armor. "Siena, you've got the next two!"

Siena nodded, on the verge of bursting out with laughter. "Ha, that's fine with me."

"If we've gone through the fire and wind elements, I guess either lightning or earth will be next." I gestured to the room above us. "Shall we find out?

We ascended the stairs to the third-floor hall. Yet again, there was a robed Druid on the dusty floor, surrounded by what looked like a laboratory. This time the Druid was pointing his hands up to the ceiling as lines of plasma struck up around his body to cover the room in glowing light.

"Tsh, any ideas for this one, smart guy?" Data asked.

"Well, I am starting to see a trend with these fights." I stepped back toward the opening, raising my arms as a hint that they should follow my lead. "The first was beaten with wind, which was also the element of the next Druid. If this is the case, one of the last starting elements would be water, right? So . . ."

When we had backed off far enough, I launched my Water Hose spell into the room, upgraded after I had used it so many times in Lucineer. The plasma began to fizzle, but it wasn't until the canopy of liquid fell upon the Druid that I remembered why you didn't want to drop anything electrical into a bathtub. He seized up, shaking violently before falling forward onto his face.

"Oh yeah, water conducts electricity, doesn't it?" Data inclined his head. "Looks like you were dead on with your elemental theory, Noah."

Siena sighed. "Alright fine, but I get the water wizard upstairs!"

"Whatever you say. I can't see how we could use Earth Punch to defeat him anyway, considering how high up from the ground we are."

We moved through the puddles and up the spiral staircase. I marveled at how far we could see now that we were near the top of the tower. The view stretched over the hills, down into the rainforest, and all the way out to the Onjira Plains. It seemed that Secotier dungeons had benefits besides higher Skill Points and items.

As we walked up the stairs onto the fourth floor and saw ancient tomes and ragged scrolls filling the dusty shelves, I knew we had reached the library, not the best place to fight a water Druid.

"Finish him off quickly," Data said.

Siena's Ruby Edge flashed into her hand, and she ran in. There was a great splash, and Data and I hid behind the wall so the water wouldn't hit us. Five minutes later, Siena appeared before us, soaking wet, her armor and hair drenched from her ponytail down to her plated greaves.

Data grinned at the reversal of the situation between them from the second floor. "What happened? Did you win?"

"Of course I won!" Siena snapped, ringing out her long ponytail. "I'd prefer not to talk about it. Let's move on."

I could see Data wanted to push his question, but Siena stalked through the room to the staircase, boots squelching with every step. I followed and heard Data snorting while trying to hold down his laughter.

This was my second dungeon with these two, and I still couldn't pinpoint their relationship. It almost seemed that they liked each other and were hiding it. But knowing Data, it was possible they just liked to tease each other. Either way, it was nice to have a friend that could do dungeons with Data.

When we were nearly at the top floor, Data's expression changed to that chin-stroking thing he seemed to like doing.

"What's wrong?"

Data shook his head. "It usually takes a party longer to get to the top of this place, and there's a pattern in this game; there's normally a set strength ratio for the dungeon's minor monsters and final boss."

"So, you're saying that because the insane Druids were easier to defeat than the Merlin Owls and other monsters from before, the final boss, this Dark Warrior, is going to be even more difficult to beat?"

He inclined his head, his expression serious. "I just can't guess how much, though. I've never fought the Dark Warrior before. I've only heard his story."

"Okay . . . ? "

"It's the generic knight falling from grace kind of thing. He had a good relationship with the Druids here until he learned of a secret in their libraries about their magic. Apparently we're supposed to be told what that secret is when we defeat him." He smirked. "Seems it'll be a promising fight."

"You get really excited about this sort of stuff, don't you? I hope it doesn't distract you from your job of instructing me."

"I don't get as excited as Siena does. You'll be fine." His brow rose skeptically at me. "You, on the other hand, I can't pin down, either. I'm not sure whether you're depressed or just cynical."

"Considering I have to fight to stop myself from going into a coma while in this game, I'd say I'm justified in being both."

"Tsh, well, I can't think of a better escape from your problems than this place," he said.

"When your whole world reminds you of that, you'd be surprised wha—"

It was ironic that, as I said this, I became lost for words when the majesty of the final floor took my breath away. The large open ceiling of the Keep seemed to spiral up like the rest of the tower. Thanks to the airflow, it was the first floor that wasn't completely covered in dust. On the stone floor was a large, round mahogany table with multiple chairs spread out around it. I first thought the table had an Arthurian vibe to it. There was a staircase behind it leading up to another stone chair on a high dais at the back of the room.

There, the Dark Warrior sat.

Chapter 18

THE DARK WARRIOR

The final boss of the Druids' Keep was in full armor, thick and heavy with large spiked shoulder guards sandwiching a Roman-style helmet with a winged visor. Skulls linked together a mantle, which a red cape flowed from and fell in layers over his breastplate. His massive sword leaned against his greaved legs, as he ground the point into the stone floor.

"He looks pretty intimidating," Siena said, hair still damp from the water Druid's attack. "Want to go first this time, Data?"

"What was it you said to me about the ratio of strength between dungeon monsters and the final boss?" I asked him.

"Yeah . . . this might be one of the more difficult bosses in Secotier. Let's play it safe. Siena, you go first. If he kills you, we'll try another way."

"Oh, how chivalrous of you!" She just shrugged and ran forward anyway.

The Dark Warrior's massive sword rose and blocked her first strike, their blades connecting with a deafening clang. The Warrior had not even left his chair. It was the first time I had seen another weapon not shatter against a full-frontal attack by a Color Blade. Siena struck twice more, and the Warrior rose slowly, parrying all the while. His armor clanked as he swung back in a long sweeping strike.

Despite only nipping Siena's avatar, it took more than a generous share of her Hit Points.

"Holy crap, this guy's one tough bastard!" Siena said.

So Datalent was right.

"Should I use a gravity spell on him? With his armor, it's got to slow him down a bit, right?"

Data threw an item at Siena that replenished her health. "You'll be risking giving him the strength to one-hit us if you give him any more weight."

"Can you think of a better plan?"

"Let him try it," Siena said. "The guy is already pretty slow. The only reason he got me was because I was overeager."

"Ha, what's new?" Data said, rolling his eyes. "Alright, launch the spell and I'll give him a try, but if I lose, get out of here as fast as you can."

"Okay." I used Gravity Pull, sending the reality-warped suppression visuals down on the dark knight. "Try to cut between the plates of his armor. Get in and get out as fast as you can."

He chuckled. "You? Giving *me* advice?"

"Well, you haven't fought this guy before, have you?" If I'd had more time to think about it, this would've been the point that I should've stepped back and said, *That's why fighting him is a really bad idea!* Instead, I said, "Siena, try to get his back!"

"Already on it!"

Siena dashed in behind the knight. He tried to turn and stalled, as though surprised that he was now moving a lot more sluggishly than before. I knew that would be his weakness. If we could watch for whenever the Dark Warrior lifted his blade, we would have nothing to worry about.

"I'll go in first from the front," Data called as the Dark Warrior spun back to meet him. "Stab your blade under his helmet when we clash, understand?"

Siena didn't reply, only watched as the large sword swung up at Data when he closed in, still at a considerable speed. Data struck down on the back of the blade with his Sapphire Edge. I could see the Dark Warrior's arms visibly tremble as he was forced to try lifting it against the weight of both my spell and Data's own force. Still, as Siena charged in to stab through his armor, the blade began to rise.

"Noah! Use a gravity spell on me!" Data yelled as he struggled against the Dark Warrior's might.

I used another Gravity Pull and watched as the animation centered on Data this time, adding weight to his blade and helping him to lower it against the Warrior's. Siena slid her blade inside his armor, stabbing deep into his flesh. A strike, even from such a rare weapon, took only a tenth of his health. The Dark Warrior seemed to grow stronger against my spell as his Hit Points went down, and he spun, disengaging from Data and swinging his sword out at Siena in a counterattack.

Siena jumped back, diverting the Warrior's attention just enough that Data could swing down his own heavy blade onto the helmet. The plated armor caved against the blade, but then stuck. There was a grunt, and the Dark Warrior swung his sword faster than my gravity spell should have let him. Data flew back from the attack, his Hit Points dropping all the way down to the red.

Data wheezed and fell to one knee. "It actually hurts!"

"That vest is the only reason you're still alive," Siena said, coming to his side.

He smiled. "Tsh, then all of my farming wasn't a waste of time, after all."

There were clanging stomps as the Dark Warrior came upon us. The way he moved now made me think that my spell had already worn off. I cast another with only half of my Mana remaining. I then unequipped my Dragon Arm. If I was going to fight him I was going to need all of the speed I could muster.

Siena caught my eyes. "Noah, don't think ab—"

I grinned at her. "At times like these, I don't think."

Crystal Blades formed in my hands. I knew my time was limited, so I quickly went to work when I knew he couldn't keep up. Like a magician inserting swords into the box his assistant was lying in, I went about stabbing Crystal Blades into the Dark Warrior's armor. Each time I broke them off, sharp shards of ice fell to the stone floor before I summoned another to thrust into him. Although it didn't do nearly as much damage as either Siena's or Data's attacks, the sheer quantity I managed to get in was enough for his health to lower by a third.

Then my gravity spell on him ran out, and I was backhanded away from the giant knight. I hit the stone, his gauntleted blow alone more than halving my health. Arachnid Silk Robes may have been one of the best Spellcaster garments in Basetier, but they provided mediocre defense against bosses in Secotier. There was no way I could hope to stand up against another attack from him.

Then my foot slid beneath me, and I saw the ice from my blades was still on the ground. I couldn't understand why they hadn't vanished like the blades I had pierced him with. Then it hit me: the Ice Regeneration ability summoned weapons of ice, the remnants of which my Wind Blast spell should be able to manipulate.

Can spells really work like that? Heck, there's only one way to find out!

As the Dark Warrior loomed over me, raising his blade, I focused on the shards and used my spell. The shards of ice shot at the knight, bursting into his armor in a cloud of Diamond Dust. They each only took minor amounts of health, but together they accumulated to cut away a good chunk of it. Then, from the cloud of dust, Siena jumped out and struck the Dark Warrior right through his visor.

The armor began to rattle violently. Siena somersaulted backwards as it began to fall from his body, one plate at a time. The man beneath the armor had a thick body and long blonde hair. He stepped out from the plates as though waking from a daze, his wide eyes wandering around the room. He looked upon us and stopped. His expression changed to a look of pain, yet he was still smiling. He then vanished in a flash of light.

Siena stood over his armor. "What? Was that it?"

I sighed and relaxed back on the stone floor. Data walked over and offered a hand to help me up. I took it, a Willow Bark in his grasp returning my health to a comfortable level as he lifted me to my feet. Obviously, the gravity spell I had cast on him had finally faded as well.

"Even I can say that that was a hard one," he said, patting me on the shoulder. "You pulled more than your own weight against him."

"Is that supposed to be a joke?"

His lips stretched into a smile. "Tsh, yeah."

"Okay, okay," Siena said as though brushing it off as nothing. "How about we do what we came here for? I'm more interested in what the reward is for this new dungeon than stroking Noah's ego."

I laughed. Unlike Data, she had seen my Crystal Blade strategy before in the Goblin Dungeon and was no longer impressed. She was right though, we did come here for a reason.

I looked around. "Where is the Cursed Pool supposed to be anyway?"

"Before all this, you had to defeat the Principal Druid before you could get into the pool. If I recall correctly, it should still be through the hidden wall behind his chair." Data pointed to the stone chair the Dark Warrior had been sitting on before the fight. "Did the Dark Warrior claim it after he made them all go insane?"

"We still don't know what caused that."

Siena walked up the stairs and behind the chair, pushing at the fake wall that swung back at her touch. "Open sesame," she said dramatically and then gestured for us to follow her into the darkness.

We followed her inside. It was more like a cave than a room. Light reflected from the pool on the room's dark ceiling. Being so high above any natural source of water was enough to tell us that the pool was mystical.

"I heard before that this is where the Druids got their magic and that their power came from madness," Data began.

I went into my menu and pulled out the Ironwood shaft he had cut for me from the Onjira Rainforest. I knelt down to dip it into the black waters.

Data continued, "I have a feeling this is what the Dark Warrior used to make the Druids go insane."

Siena snorted a laugh. "You mean he forced them all to go skinny-dipping in this place?"

"It only makes sense considering how out of control their magic was." I pulled the staff up.

— Acquired Cursed Druid Staff! —

We had completed our original goal, but after everything I had heard about the Dark Warrior's story, my curiosity got the better of me.

"But why? What was the Dark Warrior's motive for doing such a thing?"

Data shrugged. "Tsh, who knows? It doesn't seem like the answers will just be given to us after the battle like I was told. The Lucineer dungeon had some of the tale on a secret scroll. There are new stories being written and added to this world every day."

I put the staff back into my items and turned to leave the pool's cave. "If you ever meet the writer of the Dark Warrior's story, you should tell him that making a story complex by leaving out vital information is bad storytelling."

Data climbed the rocks after me, smiling. "Maybe so, but the mystery sure does attract a big audience."

Siena scoffed. "Are you guys arguing about lore? What a bunch of geeks!"

"Says the girl who's playing a fantasy game," Data said.

"I'd play a game of chess if it was as exciting as this place. I wouldn't care what its backstory is so long as I can have fun, and nothing's more fun than the feeling of life-threatening peril."

"Unlike you, however, the peril I'm facing isn't an illusion. My life is literally on the line here."

Siena grinned. "That makes me respect you even more, Noah."

I accepted different strokes for different folks and all of that, but the fact that Siena didn't like a good mystery just baffled me. Heck, I was already forming my own theory about the Dark Warrior's origin. I guess I would just have to wait until I was good enough to do that Tertiatier dungeon Data had mentioned.

Chapter 19

WHO TO CHOOSE?

The three of us made our way to the Onjira Synth Square where I could have the Night Down Robes synthesized.

The town of Onjira was similar to Yarburn. It also had a river running through it, but Onjira's river was muddy, and the houses on either side of the river were in stark contrast. The houses closer to the desert were mostly thatched and boxed huts with frayed curtains blowing in the wind. The side closer to the rainforest had taller buildings that looked like Egyptian palaces, surrounded by lush greenery. Even the smells were different, like a bed of roses versus a landfill. The garbage smell seemed to be coming from the people on the desert side, all thin and wearing tattered clothing. I tried to keep my distance as we hurried to the river.

"I don't get it. Why did the designers put NPCs that look like they are suffering in this place?"

"It's supposed to send a message to the players," Data said. "That there's a whole world out there, and while this is a place of escapism, it will remind people that there are those still suffering in the real world."

"Well, when I finally get out of here, I'll probably look as skinny as those people anyway. I've been getting dizzy spells every time I use the Gateways. My brain must not be getting enough energy to be stable in this world."

"Tsh, unlikely," Data said.

"Well, all this talk is depressing," Siena said, hair whipping around. "Tell me when you plan on having fun again."

"I guess I could tell you about my plan to go into a Tertiatier dungeon later."

Siena grinned. "Now you're talking! I look forward to it!"

Having said this, she vanished from the town square. I'd heard that having the option to log off come up without going to a Gateway was an available plugin, but I had a hunch that her appearing and disappearing wasn't due to that. I was sure she knew a way to move from place to place freely without a Transfer Orb.

Fortunately, the Synth Square was on the side of the rainforest. Thick green bushes surrounded the tracks, although there was the occasional patch of hardpan like dots on a Dalmatian. Walking into a weaver's store that resembled a Persian rug shop, I had my robes synthesized and was once again given the color option. This time, I went with my first instinct and chose black.

Despite how much help Data had been, I was somewhat relieved when he started expressing his own urge to leave.

"I know it's not really fair on you," Data said, "but just because you can't move doesn't stop the need in others. I'm not going to make an excuse to get some reality in me before preparing you for a Tertiatier dungeon."

His eyes went distant, looking at his menu.

"You don't have to make excuses. If I could move around,

I would too." I turned away from him.

"You're doing well, even without me. I would suggest playing through some more Primatier dungeons with your friends. The Tranquil Grotto is the perfect place to raise your Skill Points and get some support spells."

"I'll check it out."

He nodded and said, "Be sure you do," before vanishing, leaving me alone.

Passing the Wanted Board, I was shocked to see my name at the top of the Druids' Keep Survival Records. We had only been in the Druids' Keep for a couple of hours. If *I* received a Wanted rank there, I could only assume that my Survival Record had gotten a massive boost from the time I had accumulated in both Basetier and Primatier without ever logging off. I couldn't imagine that any other player had ever spent so much time in Basetier, and after the time conversion in Primatier, my accumulated time must have been through the roof.

Pulling up my menu to check the specs of my new equipment, I was startled by how much my own stats had increased. My Night Down Robe had high magic defense, and when added to my Dragon Arm, it increased my regular defense by a lot as well. Because of my time in Lucineer, my cold tolerance was still high, although I had no idea if this would help me fight the water elementals in the Tranquil Grotto, let alone if it would benefit me in the Tertiatier dungeon, which was my end goal. Perhaps Data would know.

Considering my Cursed Druid Staff was acquired in a Secotier dungeon, I wasn't surprised by its high stats. Data knew his weapons well enough to pick one that would make my attack combination more powerful. The staff's effects would increase the time of my gravity spell and make my Crystal Blade and Ice Regeneration combo work for longer. As I considered how to use my new abilities, I realized that if I could get the speed support magic that Keri had, I could increase the efficiency of my attack even more.

This alone was reason enough to pull up her chat. Like with Chloe, I knew I would have to tell Keri about Sue and why I was trying to enter a Tertiatier dungeon sooner or later, and what better time than when doing a dungeon together.

I said: "Hey Keri," and the message was converted into text.

She returned with: "Hi Noah! XD"

"I just wanted to apologize for how we parted in Yarburn and say that, if it weren't for your speed support magic, I wouldn't have made it out of that fight alive."

"That's alright! I was surprised when Chloe told me that you made it out at all."

"Still, it really helped with my tactics. I was wondering where it was you got that support magic."

"The Grotto. Do you want me to take you there?"

Is that the same place Data just brought up?

"Sure."

"Okay, meet me at the Galrinth Gateway in ten minutes."

I put away the chat and made my way to the Onjira Gateway. It wasn't far off from the Synth Square, and it took me only five minutes to get there by foot, even though I had to cross to the desert side of the river. I hurried past the dilapidated roads and houses, where stray animals looked for scraps.

At this point, I just wanted to get out of Onjira and head back to the cool air of Galrinth.

I went into the menu, selected the city, and jumped with

a head-pounding pulse from an Ancient African-themed setting to a romanticized Medieval European one.

Sweet Keri was there waiting for me. Her eyes lit up when she saw me, and for half of an instant, an image of Sue flashed across my mind.

I'm going to see Sue again soon.

"Have you been waiting long?"

She shook her white-hooded head.

"Alright, so what's the closest town to this dungeon?"

"All support magic can be found around the shores of Yarburn." She walked up and activated the Gateway. "I guess we can continue the date that got interrupted by that hooded guy."

I gave her a skeptical smile, trying to brush off her words. "Was that a date?"

"I'm not sure, you did kiss Chloe afterwards," she said just before she vanished.

I froze, taken aback by her nonchalant tone, then quickly followed her. Vision tunneling, I appeared in the familiar tropical town of Yarburn. Keri was already halfway down the first dune, following a sandy pathway. I caught up with her as seagulls circled above us in the warm air.

"You know she kissed *me,* right?" I corrected her. "Not the other way 'round."

"She told me you weren't expecting it." She nodded and broke into a grin. "At least going by the face she said you made afterwards."

I sighed in relief. At least that was one less thing to feel guilty about. "Wow, you guys are really open with each other." I wondered inwardly if Chloe told her about Sue and the accident, though Chloe didn't seem like someone who would gossip about something shared in confidence like that.

She tittered. "Well, we are best friends. Long-lasting relationships need transparency and understanding."

"You're not kidding." I shook my head, amazed at her jovial mood. "Okay, good, she didn't misrepresent my intentions then. But what was she thinking just kissing me like that?"

"Maybe she did it to stake a claim on you," Keri said. "I don't know whether it's because she actually likes you or just doesn't want you to take me away from her."

I took a minute to digest that. We walked past shacks and huts similar in design to the hovels in Onjira. Yet here the NPCs made it look like a place of vacation. Passing them, we made our way across the beach, and Keri continued leading me down the sand in the opposite direction of last time.

I had originally thought Chloe hated me and Keri was interested in me, but if Chloe kissing me didn't bother her, maybe I'd been reading that wrong. I had only been getting a commentary of Chloe's emotions after all.

"So, how do you feel about . . . you know?" I asked.

"I, uh . . . look!" She pointed to the Gateway that appeared where the sand of the beach met the water. "The dungeon's up there!"

I couldn't let her dodge the subject. I'd let this go on long enough. "You and Chloe are still friends, right?"

"Yeah. I think she's just confused about how she feels, and she hates that."

I nodded, but that didn't really get to the point of what I wanted to know. "I guess the real question is . . . what do you want from me?"

"I don't know. Let's just have fun, okay?"

We moved to the Gateway, a circle of green-blue light hovering above the sand. We brought up the menu to go to the Primatier dungeon. I was amused that the title was indeed the Tranquil Grotto.

Data has more foresight than I gave him credit for.

I used the Key Trigger option, and we vanished from the bay, reappearing in a cool area away from the beach. We were in a deep cave with water crashing around its rocks in shallow pools.

Chapter 20

MORE THAN FRIENDS

Of all the dungeons in this game, Tranquil Grotto seemed the least likely to have earned that label. The areas were beautiful and refreshingly cool after being in the tropical humidity of Yarburn and the desert heat of Onjira. I followed the cave path out into the light, hearing waves crashing outside.

Wow, Sue would love this place. She was always insisting we go on walks along the beach during the summer. It was just a short drive from her house. We had spent hours there, just the two of us, when we'd first started dating. We'd even talked about getting a place close to the shore after graduation. *Maybe I can show her after I get her out of here.*

I emerged into a small cove. Glowworms stuck to the ceiling in parts of the cave, illuminating the waterworn rock in green light. Green slime and seaweed covered the stone pillars that the waves splashed up against, with a sand pathway leading out to a glaring opening of coastal cliffs. The path continued out onto a rocky shore, with long green vines dangling down from an overhanging clay gorge. Keri was standing atop it, looking out at the ocean. Seeing me, she ran down from where the rock path led, took my hand, and tugged me back into the cool shadows of the cave.

"First things first," she said in a jumble of words so fast I almost couldn't keep up. "I'll take you to the place where you need to do the mini-game to get Speed Amp." She seemed nervous.

"Do I have to do anything serious? Like, are there any monsters to fight?"

"There are monsters around here somewhere, but they're weak, and this won't involve them." She let go of me and ran ahead. "I'll show you when we get there."

I really couldn't understand how this place was a Primatier dungeon. Not only did it look like just another part of the Yarburn coast, but we hadn't been swamped with any enemies or PvP opponents yet. Apparently, there were no Chaos Engines and no random encounters here. It seemed like the whole point of this place was a relatively safe space to help the players who wanted only to support their teammates. It was rather anticlimactic but also calming.

"I hope you don't mind how boring this place is," she said as we walked through the dark tunnels. She had to talk loudly over the echoes of the waves hitting the rocks. "You can't even win a Wanted rank here."

"I don't mind. After what I've been doing lately, I really needed to do something relaxing."

"I love this place." She spun to take it all in but then gave me a mischievous grin.

"I'm sure you do. I've heard it's the best place to get support magic, so I can imagine how helpful it is for you."

"Are you claustrophobic or afraid of drowning?"

I laughed nervously. "Isn't everyone a little?"

"I'll take that as a yes. A fear of drowning will help you get the Speed Amp spell."

"How's that?"

The cave took a turn that went further down into the darkness. Waves crashed high against the stone barrier at the entrance, spraying us with saltwater. I could only guess what would happen next.

"In order to get the speed support magic, all you need to do is run down that tunnel before the water can catch up with you," she said.

"What happens if I don't make it in time?"

"You drown."

That would be a major problem.

She seemed to recognize my expression. "But I've seen you move, you easily have the stamina to make it! You just have to have a little faith in me."

"More than a little."

"You have to do this to get Speed Amp." She rolled her eyes. "But I suppose I'll go first to show you that someone with lower speed than you can do it easily. I'll see you on the other side."

She lifted the skirts of her white robe and took off into the tunnel. I watched in shock as the stone barrier lowered and the tide rose over it, the water rushing into the tunnel. I could see right away why she had also asked me if I was claustrophobic. Most people would have a fear of water rising in a place you couldn't escape from.

I'm here for Sue. Keri is trustworthy.

As soon as the barrier rose again and the tide lowered, I removed my armor to give me more speed. Waiting until the water became as low as possible, I limbered up and took off into the tunnel, sprinting through the darkness as fast as I could. The first thing I hadn't realized was that the pitch-blackness would stop me from seeing where I was going. I just kept running, hoping there weren't any branching tunnels that I could get lost in.

I saw a light ahead of me and first thought it was the end of the tunnel, but then recognized it as a floating item. Confused why Keri hadn't taken it, I grabbed the glowing object on my way past, barely giving it a passing glance.

— Acquired Torn Note Piece! —

Despite my surprise, the sound of rushing water approached from behind me, spurring me on. I picked up my pace. My breaths pumped in my chest, but whether from fear or from exerting my avatar, I didn't have time to think about it. I just wanted to get out of here before the roaring water behind me could catch up. As I felt my back begin to catch the first drops of the spray, I saw the true light at the end of the tunnel and bolted toward it.

The air pressure from the tunnel pushed at my back as soon as I exited the tunnel. I must have stopped before I should have because the water flew up from behind me, drenching my robes.

Keri's laughter echoed through the cave. "I got a bit wet too," she said.

After I waved my arms to fling off some of the drops, I

looked up to see her . . . and stopped. Having unequipped her wet robes, she was now only wearing plain white undergarments, which I guessed was her avatar's default appearance. When she noticed I was staring, she hunched her shoulders and turned so I could only see her in profile, hands clasped timidly at her chest.

"Your clothes dry automatically if you unequip them for a while," she said.

At this inconvenient moment, the window popped up.

— Ability to learn Speed Amp unlocked! —

It was hard not to pay attention to Keri. She was beautiful and slenderer than her spellcaster robes had suggested. With her robe unequipped, I could see her long blonde hair that had been covered by her hood.

Just here for a spell, huh? Who am I fooling?

However, being in a game, the whole situation had me feeling suspicious.

"I don't suppose you'd be offended if I ask if you changed your avatar to look like that? I know the Dream Engine can read faces, but other than that . . ."

"Are you asking if I'm a girl in real life? I guess Chloe and I could be guys for all you know."

That was an uncomfortable thought.

"I'm joking!" She laughed nervously. "Besides, this is my own voice you're hearing. I don't sound like a guy, do I?"

Pulling my eyes away from her, I moved to an opening in the tunnel and out onto the rocks. I had another Torn Note Piece to worry about.

Did Bitcon leave it there? It didn't make sense that he

would have known I was coming here. *Was finding one right after defeating him just a coincidence?*

Sitting on a boulder, I accessed my items and brought it up. It read:

> *It's perpetually night in this place, and it's been nearly two weeks since I last saw the sun. They allow me to move around now, but no matter where I go, I can't find an exit. Every time I move into another room, the whole building shakes and suddenly where the ground floor had been is now two floors up in the air. I dare not jump from such a height, but I fear that if I don't, I will be trapped in here forever. I've waited so long since the accident, but with each passing day, my heart grows colder.*

Guilt tugging at my heart, I looked out over the shore as my robe dried off in the sun. Keri sat beside me. Her blonde hair was caught by the wind and curled around her shoulders. She looked beautiful, but after what I had just read, it was merely salt in the wound of my betrayal.

She re-equipped her Spellcaster robes, concern in her expression. "Are you okay?"

I didn't know what to say. *The only reason I'm doing this is because I'm planning to rescue my girlfriend?*

I shook my head. "Worrying what you really look like is kind of ironic considering right now I'm stuck in a hospital bed, malnourished, with a nurse having to wipe my butt and force feed me through a tube. This doesn't include the amount of therapy I'm going to have to do when I wake up, and here I am, worried about if you're as attractive as you've made your avatar."

Keri shrugged. "Do you really think the real world means that much to me? I choose to have this life." She turned her gaze out toward the ocean. "Will you remain in this game once you've recovered? Or will the real world take priority?"

"I . . . don't know, at least not until I wake up. For now, it's all I have to hold out for. It's one of the reasons I want to get stronger. Besides, there is a girl . . ."

My main reason to gain spells and Skill Points was that I wanted to rescue Sue. But I thought maybe this would be enough to make sure Keri didn't get the wrong idea about our time together. I didn't want to lose her completely.

I continued, "I can't express how terrified I am that I might not get to experience real life one more time. Even if . . ."

Keri sighed and stood from the rock. "Then there's no point in us being here. Until you're sure you're not just going to disappear with someone else one day, I'm not going to flip a coin and see what side it lands on."

I winced at the description. It was more accurate than she knew. But her words made me nervous. *Was she not going to be around me at all until I decided?*

"That's fair enough," I said, wanting to make sure I wasn't leading her on with my next question. "But can we still play together as friends?"

She nodded and, although she was smiling, her voice had turned cold as she said, "Only if you don't go for Chloe during your time here, either. I won't have you hurting her."

"That makes sense." It really did. "I'm not a complete scoundrel, you know?"

She turned her face away so I couldn't see her expression. "I know. I wouldn't have come here with you if I thought you were. We . . ." She breathed out a painful sigh before saying in an understanding voice, "We all get lonely sometimes."

She then vanished from the rocks, and I was left alone to curse the world and the situation it had put me in. I could tell that I wasn't the only one of us who had been burnt by a relationship in the past. But unlike her, I wasn't going to just leave Sue as a thing of the past.

I'm wasting time. I have to get stronger!

Chapter 21

SKY ISLAND

After getting the third Torn Note Piece, I knew I had to call and confirm what I now knew with my mother. I figured she might be able to contact the Wona Company and get Sue some help. However, when she appeared in the video feed, she looked even more haggard than usual.

"Dear, I've got some bad news."

I nodded. "I've got good news, so let me go first. Sue's in here, Mom. I've been getting in-game letters from her."

My mother looked down, pinching the bridge of her nose. "That's impossible, dear."

"It's not. I know she's in here!"

"Sue died yesterday in the early morning." My mother sighed and shook her head. "I tried to get in contact with you earlier, but you weren't responding."

My breath hitched, the cold darkness filling me again. "No, but yesterday . . ."

"Her heart stopped during the night, and they were unable to resuscitate her."

"That means . . ."

That means that a part of her managed to get into the game beforehand. That's why they can keep her trapped in one place. If I could just find her, then maybe . . . maybe she won't be lost to me.

"Noah?" I could hear the stress and exhaustion in her words.

"I see . . . I need to be alone for a little while."

My mother nodded. "I understand. Remember that I'm right here if you ever need to talk."

"I know . . . bye."

Sue wasn't dead. The letters proved that a part of her was still trapped in Tertiatier . . . but I wasn't strong enough to save her yet!

I found myself a brutal Primatier dungeon to take my frustrations out on. I tried to message Brock, but he didn't respond. He must have been frustrated when he saw my Wanted ranks in both a Primatier and Secotier dungeon even after he had warned me to try and avoid them.

Siena did mention that the dungeon had been updated recently, but still . . .

I couldn't call any of my other friends in. It was one thing to be just friends with Keri and another to have her around when Sue was trapped in the game forever. Considering how I had last left Chloe, I couldn't call her either. And their apparent transparency meant doing a dungeon with David was out of the question as well.

So, instead, I entered the dungeon on my own. It was another Toena dungeon called the Haunted Shrine, and with my new support magic, I could move through it by myself without too much trouble.

The game designers really went out of their way to make the place as scary as possible by using eerie background music with the occasional scream and tinting everything in dark green. Candles floated in the halls, and shadows that appeared behind the rice paper walls would vanish when I slid open the doors.

About as scary as the haunted house during the nighttime carnival I took Sue to.

The Haunted Shrine was possessed mostly with Ghost monsters, the majority of which I could only defeat with spells or magical weapons. Screaming Ghosts of robed monks and priestesses rushed toward me, each of them with the regular strength of Primatier monsters. I killed one with a Fire Weave, and it let out a haunting scream as my Skill Points and Moola jumped high enough to get me the Speed Amp spell.

Using my new Druid Staff, not only did my Gravity Pull spell slow the monsters for longer, but after using it enough times, I received Gravity Well. The tutorial avatar held both hands in a V-shape to direct the spell, raising and then lowering their arms. Gravity Well affected all of the monsters within range, the warping animation showing the exact monsters affected so I could make quick work of them with my Crystal Blades.

I might have been scared of the ghosts if I wasn't so angry with myself.

I charged down a long corridor, blasting my way through the phantoms until I came to the final room. When I entered, the rice paper door slammed shut behind me. I turned to open it, but it turned to stone, completely jammed. I was trapped.

When I turned to find another way out, I saw the dungeon's boss. A Kanji scroll clearly announced it as a

"Wailing Wall." The far side of the room advanced while a horrific face in the wall moaned. Bony arms protruded from the red wallpaper and flailed about. The dust on the floor's planks piled up where the wall creaked across them, the rest of the shrine seeming to groan with it.

I charged in and, trying to avoid its swinging arms, I struck at it with my Crystal Blades. I thought I was doing adequate damage as it crept toward me, not losing any Hit Points myself. It wasn't until I saw the wall behind me coming closer that I realized the Wailing Wall had a time limit to defeat it. It seemed that if you didn't kill it by the time it reached the back wall, you would be crushed.

I sped up my attacks, hacking and slashing, taking a decent chunk out of its Hit Points. I thought I could still finish it off without resorting to using my Transfer Orb. Yet when the distance I had left to move was less than three meters, fear rose in me.

I was pulling up my menu when another player appeared at my side. With a final devastating slash, he rid the Wailing Wall of the remaining tenth of its hit points.

As it vanished in another piercing wail, a window appeared in my vision with the usual achievement fanfare.

— Ability to learn Illusion unlocked! —

Wondering what this new spell did or even what I had done to achieve it, I turned to the player who had helped me. I didn't know if the assistance was because he thought I needed help, or because he simply wanted a share of the Skill Points, but I was grateful either way. I was shocked to recognize the familiar, cold-eyed, Elven face of Sirswift, holding his massive sword aloft before him.

At first, I was speechless, confused as to why such a famous player would come to my aid.

This is a Primatier dungeon. What's he even doing here?

"Uh . . . thanks?" I said.

He rose from his final attack. "A short demonstration of the difference between our abilities."

I shrugged. "Well, you are a Heavy, and they are naturally inclined to do more damage with physical attacks. Besides, a few more hits and I would've finished it off by myself anyway."

He raised a brow at me. "You'll never reach Tertiatier if that's what you think."

I balled my fists in frustration. The boss had only had a few Hit Points remaining. Besides, Sirswift came into the battle at the last minute but acted like he had done the entire dungeon with me only holding him back.

"So, why are you here anyway?" I asked. "Shouldn't someone as good as you be grinding in Tertiatier with your other Wanted-ranked buddies?"

"Data sent me into this place to retrieve you. He tried to message you, but you weren't replying. He ran into me in Toena and thought I would retrieve you quicker, as though that justifies me being his errand boy. You wouldn't send Superman to get eggs and milk at the speed of light, would you?"

Even I couldn't tell if I was shaking my head more at his bitter tone or his over-the-top analogy. "What does Data want me for?"

"Something to do with getting you a flying mount to get to the Penance Peaks Gateway." Sirswift turned to leave the Haunted Shrine, and I followed him out. "Then again, I don't see the point. You won't be able to get past the kind of monsters that guard a Tertiatier Gateway."

I clenched my jaw and said, "We'll see about that."

Sirswift smirked. "You should really alter your menu's settings so that you can receive messages during dungeons."

That explains why my mother couldn't get in contact with me before.

"How do I do that?"

He shook his head as though baffled. "Use your configuration settings, obviously."

I went through my menus and found the option. It really was as simple as turning the message warnings during dungeons from off to on, which made me feel a little sheepish.

The shrine's many stone-tiled steps led down to a dirt track that became less distinct as it faded into the fields of Toena. I spotted Data leaning against a black archway at the bottom, waiting for us.

He gave me a smile in greeting and said, "I was thinking about saving this for last as it's one of the more fun things to do in this world, but I guess if you have to do a quest in Tertiatier, you might as well travel there in style."

I lifted a brow. "Where are we going?"

Sirswift waggled his fingers dramatically and said, "It's a surprise."

After spending so much time with Data, I thought I had gotten used to such petty sarcasm. I was wrong.

We used the Gateway to go to a place called Sky Island. The name was a dead giveaway, but when we arrived, even my annoyance at Sirswift couldn't ruin my awe of the place.

Enormous clouds streaked the blue sky right above us. High green hills filled one side of the hovering island. A waterfall ran over one of the hill's cliff faces, forming a river that cut through the green brush. Upon reaching the other edge of the island, the water tumbled over the side and down the steep drop onto the Penance Mountains below. I didn't have the slightest idea where the water came from, but that didn't make the sight any less beautiful.

Maybe it was because players couldn't see past the dark clouds above the Penance Peaks, but there were more flying beasts perched here than I had seen in all of Basetier.

Data waved at them. "See? Take your pick."

"Not everyone has a Hero rank guardian to get them through a Secotier dungeon," Sirswift said. "Consider yourself lucky that you get access to this privilege."

I barely heard him as I gazed at the flying monsters. Dragons, Fire Birds, large Vampire Bats, Griffins, Hippogriffs, Air Rexes, and any number of shining monsters soared through the clouds before coming in to land on the hills. We paced up the rocky pathway, Data naming the mounts I didn't recognize and Sirswift criticizing their qualities.

I knew which one I wanted as soon as I saw it. The closest thing I could compare it to was a Pegasus, but with dragon wings and lion-like legs. It seemed to radiate with neon-blue lightning, the perfect steed for a Spellcaster. As I approached it, it neighed at me, and the flapping of its dragon wings caused the wind to blow in my eyes.

— Peragon —

"I want that one."

Sirswift let out a "pffft!"

I furrowed my brow, beginning to get sick of his attitude.

"What?"

He laughed. "That's like a homeless man saying he wants a diamond ring. You have to beat it by yourself if you want to get its Summoning Stone."

Data inclined his head, rubbing his chin. "Tsh, he's right, Noah."

"Is there a Synth Square in this place?" I asked.

Data nodded and led me to the square as Sirswift kept an eye on the Peragon. This Synth Square was surrounded by holes that dropped out into open space. I supposed it was only fitting for a place called Sky Island.

I headed for the spell shop, paid for the Speed Amp and Illusion spells with my now-sufficient supply of Moola, and performed the light ceremony as quickly as I could. I made a beeline back to where Sirswift and the neon-blue mount waited for us.

I was determined to take it back to Basetier with me.

"Ha, good luck," Sirswift said with not a hint of well-wishing in his voice.

I went to work. First, I brought out my Druid Staff, casting Speed Amp on myself. I then made the arm-lowering gesture to cast a Gravity Well on the Peragon so it wouldn't fly off. Sending an Ice Wall behind it so it couldn't back away from me, I ran in. It reared up to attack, but I was now fast enough to catch its claws on my Dragon Arm. It still did enough damage to make me concerned, but before it could rise for another, I had already struck several times with a few Crystal Blades, taking out more than half of its health.

I backed off and heard Data whistle as though impressed. If I had spent more Skill Points on raising my strength during my training, this fight would have been over quicker, but I'd prioritized the defensive speed stats instead. It was a worthwhile trade. I had worked my butt off, but I felt I was finally as fast as a Spellcaster could get in Primatier.

That's when the Peragon charged at me. It was still pinned down by my Gravity Well, so I dropped the Crystal Blades and pulled out my Druid Staff, launching a Fire Weave at it. Its Hit Points dropped into the red zone before it could reach me, and all it took was one more slash with a Crystal Blade to finish it off.

You're mine!

It reared up once more before it dropped to the ground. Like many monsters, the Peragon dropped an item when it vanished. I picked up the blue stone.

— Acquired Summoning Stone for Peragon! —

My companions both watched my celebratory fist pump silently, Data grinning, Sirswift looking like he'd just eaten a particularly sour lemon.

Data shook his head. "Wow, that was, uh . . ."

"I told you, I wanted him."

"Tsh, I mean . . ." He stopped and shook his head again. "I just wasn't expecting you to finish it off so quickly! Come on, Swifty, that was pretty impressive!"

Sirswift shrugged. "He used surprisingly few spells for a Spellcaster."

It seemed this was the best praise I was going to get from him.

"Don't underestimate people who literally haven't had a life outside the game for three weeks straight." I felt it was time to ask what I needed to know. "So, if you need a mount to get to the top of the Penance Mountains, how will I be able to get a party up there with me?"

"Once you've been to a place you can use your Transfer Orb to bring a party with you," Data said, glancing away.

"How did you know I had one?"

"Siena told me."

I rolled my eyes. "Of course."

"You know, those items are incredibly expensive." Sirswift's voice grew suddenly intense. "How did you manage to get your hands on one?"

I caught his narrowing eyes. "It was a gift from a friend."

Sirswift grinned. "Oh . . . I see."

Data shrugged. "I think you can get it organized with the others now. It's a Saturday in three days in the real world, so get in contact with them before they plan something else during that time."

I nodded. "Alright, but before that, I want to ride this thing."

I pulled out the Summoning Stone, and the option to summon the Peragon appeared in my Key Triggers. I selected it, and with a flash, my mount appeared overhead and flapped its massive wings to land in front of me. Having never ridden a horse before, let alone one this big, being able to jump six feet helped me get onto its back. I marveled at how lifelike it was as I stroked its thick neck, which vibrated with each breath. In one of my more unoriginal moments, instead of coming up with a new name for my mount, I just started calling it *Peragon*.

"So, how do I ride this thing?"

"It moves to the areas you're focusing on, so try not to

look at things you don't want to fly into," Data said.

I looked around but nothing happened. "Alright, but how do I get it into the air?"

"Uh, I dunno, you might want to try touching it," Sirswift said.

Despite his attitude, I almost wanted to thank him for his help. At this point, I would have taken advice from anyone if it meant being able to fly away from his patronizing voice. I wondered how he had so many friends, but I guessed when it came to having skilled people in your team, beggars couldn't be choosers.

I patted Peragon's smooth side and held on tight as it reared up. With the way that its spine was shaped, it felt like I was sitting on a rocking bike seat. Wings flapping, Peragon rose into the air, taking me with it.

"Hey!" I heard Data's voice through the sudden rush of wind as I ascended. "Some areas of the sky have flying monsters!"

I barely registered what he said. We shot up through the nearby clouds, gliding over Sky Island and off into the open blue.

I looked over my shoulder, and Peragon turned sharply, forcing me to hold on more tightly so I wouldn't fall off. From on high, the island looked like an iceberg floating in the ocean of the sky. The hills of Sky Island were tall enough to cut through the clouds overhead. A rainbow arched over the entire island, and I swore I could see its mountainous, rocky underside from this far away.

I really hoped Data and Sirswift weren't planning on waiting for me there. With the amount of aerial exploring I had to do, I wasn't going to be coming back anytime soon.

I had to give it to Data, flying was a great way of cheering up my day . . . even if it wasn't actually daytime in the real world.

Chapter 22
GUILT

Peragon swooped down through the clouds. The gut-pulling effect of diving, the wind blowing through my hair, the amazing view of the jagged mountains stretching from Lucineer to Galrinth—it all made flying overwhelmingly fun.

Since leaving Data and Sirswift at Sky Island, I had wasted no time in exploring all of the many secret coves and picturesque shorelines around Yarburn. Again, the beaches reminded me of Sue, but when the prospect of only being able to see her in the game came to mind, I shunned it away.

Then I soared over the dark peninsula leading to Widows' Forest and Galrinth, which stretched up to the Penance Mountains. I followed the giant stone wall over the Toena hills. The closer the hills came to Yarburn beach's setting sun, the redder they appeared. Everything was different from above, and moving from place to place was much more pleasant on the back of Peragon than using the Gateways.

Deciding to see how large the Dream State was, I turned north and just kept flying. I flew through both day and night zones, traveling to areas I hadn't seen before. I flew over the Onjira desert, rainforest, and the hills that led up to the Druids' Keep. Once I passed the Keep, the sky became dark and rain began to fall from the rumbling clouds. The ground below shifted from dark wastelands to swampy marshlands. I continued into the growing storm, which was reminiscent of the blizzards I had faced in Lucineer.

When a bolt of lightning fell from the sky near me, I had to swerve Peragon. If I hadn't already had access to the lightning spell, this would probably be where I had to come to get it. Data had endowed me with the lightning spell as soon as I'd arrived because a player can't go to Sky Island to get a mount until they complete a Secotier dungeon. At the time, he'd thought I'd be staying in Basetier.

The space between the wasteland and marshland was spotted with cratered puddles, as though the lightning had blown portions out of the land, which were filled with the constant downpour.

I continued north. Through the hazy mists, I could have sworn I saw another city in the distance, but every time I tried to fly toward it, another fork of lightning cut down in front me. Startled, I whirled on Peragon, shooting off in another direction for a while before attempting to head north again. Another flash of lightning shot down from the dark clouds, and then another when I tried it further down the marshlands. Every time I tried to get closer to the city, I was intercepted by either lightning or a gust of wind too strong to fly into.

It's like there's an invisible wall here.

After an hour of testing out the limits of where I could go without being harassed by the weather, I realized that the only way to go farther would be to use a Gateway, although I had no idea of the name of the city behind the barrier. I turned my mount to find the nearest Gateway.

Before I made it out of the storm, a contact window appeared before me. I brought it up and was pleased to see that it was a message from David.

Maybe he'll know the name of that city . . .

Then I read the message: "Noah, we have to talk."

I said: "What is it?"

"This is killing me, man. I have to get something off my chest."

Being battered by winds and rain, I was too impatient to keep this up. I decided that talking to him face-to-face would be better.

"Let's meet up. Where are you now?"

"I'm farming ore for a new axe in Dangan Canyon. It's a Basetier area between the Onjira desert and Yarburn Village."

I hadn't been there before, but I thought I knew of the area he was talking about. I was almost glad that Transfer Orbs couldn't take me to places I hadn't already been, as this gave me more of a reason to explore the world. It was much more fun to explore each new area than to just jump directly from dungeon to dungeon.

"I'm north of Onjira. It'll take me a few minutes to fly there."

"You have a mount now? When did that happen?"

I smiled. "I completed the Druids' Keep with Data and Siena the other day."

"Man, you should've brought me along!"

I shook my head and put away the conversation. As I leaned forward, Peragon rocketed back in the direction I'd originally flown from. Five minutes later, I was passing back over the Onjira hills, thinking that if I flew in the direction of Yarburn I would inevitably come across the canyon.

I eventually saw it in the distance. Dangan Canyon was made up of several giant gorges and ravines that looked like deep scars in the dry land. Seeing how massive the place was, I was beginning to think maybe I should have gotten David to be a bit more specific with his directions. However, it seemed David had thought of this himself, for I spotted his massive avatar waving his arms on top of one of the tall plateaus.

My stomach rose, and adrenaline pulsed through me as I dropped down toward it but pulled up before I could splat into its flat peak. I jumped from Peragon and came to meet David, who was staring with bulging eyes at the glowing half-Pegasus, half-dragon.

"Holy crap, that's a sick mount, Noah!"

I used the Key Trigger Dismiss to return Peragon to its Summoning Stone. "I thought you'd survived a Secotier dungeon before. Why don't you get one yourself?"

David sighed, his massive body slouching. "Because the larger the mount, the more Skill Points you have to accumulate to ride it, and only the biggest mounts can support the weight of Heavies."

Sirswift's massive serpent mount suddenly made sense to me. I'd thought he had chosen it to show off.

"Ha, the creators really did pay a lot of attention to the weight system of this game's physics engine, despite letting us jump six feet into the air."

I walked to the edge of the plateau and looked down over the drop. The cliffs and trenches were layered with the many brown tones of the land's sediments, as though the creators were trying to represent the ancient age of the Dream State.

"So . . . you said you wanted to get something off your chest?"

David sighed and shook his head. "This is really hard for me, Noah, but it's been eating me up inside. I feel really bad about it."

I turned, hoping he wasn't talking about Keri, but he avoided my eyes. "Well?"

"When you came over to my place before your accident, I thought I might have been able to convince you to try out the Dream Game with me." His lips curled against his gritted teeth, but he balled his fists and continued. "So, I put some DSD in a bottle of soda and . . ."

It suddenly dawned on me.

"That was why I crashed!"

His lids were clenched tight; this really was hard for him to admit to.

"My mother said I was lucky to have connected to the Dream Engine at all. I couldn't unless I already had DSD in my system!"

"Listen, Noah, I—I really didn't mean for any of this to happen." His voice was trembling. "I—I didn't even realize what I'd done until I noticed the bottle in the recycling bin . . . I'm so sorry."

It all made sense now. I understood the gap in my memory before the crash, and why I had suddenly felt dizzy. This was the reason why I was stuck in this place.

The revelation made anger burn inside me, but not at David, at myself. I had been so stupid to take a drink without asking. And I had known I was feeling weird, but I still drove home.

It was my fault.

"I don't blame you," I finally said.

"But Noah—"

"No one forced me to drink it. I took it because I was angry that I didn't get to hang out with you like we used to. I'm so stupid!"

David came to my side. "You didn't know. If you had, you wouldn't have taken it."

"And you didn't know I was going to take it . . . but I did. You're not the one to blame, I am."

"Listen, Noah . . ." He trailed off.

I bit my lip and then forced a smile. "I guess it could have been worse. I could be dead." I didn't mention that I had reason to believe Sue was still alive in the game, or my mother's news about what had happened to her body back at the hospital. David didn't need to blame himself for any of that. "Honestly, although it doesn't make up for what happened, I've really had fun in here with all you guys."

I moved back to the center of the plateau and took out my Summoning Stone.

David followed me. "Where are you going?"

"I have to be alone for a while to think." My voice cracked as I summoned Peragon and jumped onto its back. Before I left, I asked, "Have you ever wanted to do a Tertiatier dungeon with the player who has the highest Survival Record?"

David's brow furrowed. "You mean Sirswift?"

I nodded. "Data might be able to convince him to join us in doing a dungeon soon. If he does, would you be interested in joining us too?"

His face broke out into a wide grin. "Definitely!"

"Then round up the girls and tell them to meet us in Galrinth's town square Saturday at lunch time. I'll have a Transfer Orb ready to teleport us to the Gateway."

"Will do!"

I rode with Peragon to the edge of the plateau and took off. My mind was awash with the piercing guilt of the car accident all over again. Everything that had happened to Sue was my fault.

I have to make this right. I have to find her.

Chapter 23
ALL OR NOTHING

I received a message from my mother the morning of the quest. I brought up the chat.

Her face appeared, smiling even with the gray rings under her eyes. "Hello dear! How has your week been?"

"Good," I said, putting on a brave face. "I've been catching up with friends and just trying to have fun while I'm in here."

"Well, that's good to hear, and how is everyone?"

"Great, I mean . . . they get to come and go as they please." I had managed to find an empty alley where the noise of the Galrinth crowd was low enough to hear her. "We're going on a raid today."

"Well, that's good. I've also got good news for you!" Her voice gained a tone of excitement. "It's still early stages, but the doctor says that very soon we'll be able to wake you up!"

"How soon?"

"Within the next day or two, he says."

"That's great," I said, although I wasn't sure it was. "Well, I guess I can say goodbye to this world soon."

"Yes, we can bring you home and start your rehabilitation there."

"Well . . . great." I felt my heartbeat quicken in pace, but whether it was more from excitement or the fear of leaving this world too early, I didn't know. "I suppose I will see you soon then."

"And Noah . . . about Sue."

I shook my head. "It's okay. I'll be out soon, and we can deal with it then."

Her expression told me she wanted to speak with me more, but I really needed some time to think alone before everyone showed up. As soon as she said goodbye, I removed the window from my vision.

It was hard to imagine being out of the game anymore. I'd been in here for so long. I'd found my friends again. I'd been having fun.

Plus, Sue isn't out there anymore.

Even if I left this world and recovered, it didn't mean I couldn't return one day. If anything, my mother's news had given me ample reason to be more cautious in our next mission. I knew how dangerous it would be to slip into a coma if I was defeated, and the odds of this happening in Tertiatier were much higher than in any other tier. If I did fall into a coma, even now, I could possibly never come out of it. I would have to reassess how I felt about the game once I was out and this threat wasn't looming over me.

It also meant that I had a shorter amount of time left to save Sue. I might only get one shot at this dungeon. With the clock ticking down, I had to do it now. I wasn't going to let all of my training and preparation go to waste. I turned from the dark alley and made my way down a road to exit Galrinth. I knew the bustling city like the back of my hand now, and it didn't take me long to get to the drawbridge entrance.

My first goal was to fly to the Tertiatier dungeon's Gateway. When I reached the top of Penance Peaks on my own, I could use the Transfer Orb to bring my friends back to start the dungeon.

Of those I had invited, only Chloe and Keri had tried to convince me to change my mind before agreeing to accompany me. It seemed David had been so excited about doing a dungeon with Sirswift that he had forgotten all about the consequences if I was killed there.

Once again, Brock hadn't replied to any of my messages. It confused me. Sure, it had been a long time since he, David, and I had all hung out together during high school, but he had never given me the cold shoulder like this. Either way, I had messaged him about the Torn Note Piece items and my compulsion to see what they meant.

Emerging from the high city walls into the Galrinth Fields, I brought out my blue Summoning Stone and summoned my mount. After two days of flying around and exploring the Dream State, I was now partial to riding it. Peragon appeared with a bright flash in the air overhead. It swooped into a graceful landing on the soft grass, and I hopped on. Clapping it on the back and focusing on the distant mountain peaks, I rode into the sky.

The wind picked up, causing my robe to flap behind me. The further we rose into the mountains, the colder the air became. I watched the fields pass under us, followed by the tunnels into the Penance Mines and the brush that led up into the mountains. We flew over the same "Yes, we can bring you home and start your rehabilitation there."

"Well . . . great." I felt my heartbeat quicken in pace, but whether it was more from excitement or the fear of leaving this world too early, I didn't know. "I suppose I will see you soon then."

"And Noah . . . about Sue."

I shook my head. "It's okay. I'll be out soon, and we can deal with it then."

Her expression told me she wanted to speak with me more, but I really needed some time to think alone before everyone showed up. As soon as she said goodbye, I removed the window from my vision.

It was hard to imagine being out of the game anymore. I'd been in here for so long. I'd found my friends again. I'd been having fun.

Plus, Sue isn't out there anymore.

Even if I left this world and recovered, it didn't mean I couldn't return one day. If anything, my mother's news had given me ample reason to be more cautious in our next mission. I knew how dangerous it would be to slip into a coma if I was defeated, and the odds of this happening in Tertiatier were much higher than in any other tier. If I did fall into a coma, even now, I could possibly never come out of it. I would have to reassess how I felt about the game once I was out and this threat wasn't looming over me.

It also meant that I had a shorter amount of time left to save Sue. I might only get one shot at this dungeon. With the clock ticking down, I had to do it now. I wasn't going to let all of my training and preparation go to waste. I turned from the dark alley and made my way down a road to exit Galrinth. I knew the bustling city like the back of my hand now, and it didn't take me long to get to the drawbridge entrance.

My first goal was to fly to the Tertiatier dungeon's Gateway. When I reached the top of Penance Peaks on my own, I could use the Transfer Orb to bring my friends back to start the dungeon.

Of those I had invited, only Chloe and Keri had tried to convince me to change my mind before agreeing to accompany me. It seemed David had been so excited about doing a dungeon with Sirswift that he had forgotten all about the consequences if I was killed there.

Once again, Brock hadn't replied to any of my messages. It confused me. Sure, it had been a long time since he, David, and I had all hung out together during high school, but he had never given me the cold shoulder like this. Either way, I had messaged him about the Torn Note Piece items and my compulsion to see what they meant.

Emerging from the high city walls into the Galrinth Fields, I brought out my blue Summoning Stone and summoned my mount. After two days of flying around and exploring the Dream State, I was now partial to riding it. Peragon appeared with a bright flash in the air overhead. It swooped into a graceful landing on the soft grass, and I hopped on. Clapping it on the back and focusing on the distant mountain peaks, I rode into the sky.

The wind picked up, causing my robe to flap behind me. The further we rose into the mountains, the colder the air became. I watched the fields pass under us, followed by the tunnels into the Penance Mines and the brush that led up into the mountains. We flew over the same waterfall that created the underground pools where Siena and I had fought the Golem.

Although I had seen most of the mountain's features from the fields leading up to the mines, there were still details in every nook and cranny yet to be explored. Data had warned me that I would need to look out for the flying monsters that emerged from their depths on my way to the Penance Peaks Gateway. Like Sirswift, he had also mentioned that the monsters leading up to the Tertiatier Gateway would be of harder stuff than the papier-mâché I'd been training my new spells on in Primatier.

I saw them emerge from the mountains and gasped. Clouds of Vampire Bats, flocks of large Ravens, and many other flying monsters flew at me. I used my Fire Weave spell, and lines of flame shot into them. I thought this would have done the job, but many of the creatures just flew through the flames. Using it a few more times, I managed to kill off the weaker creatures, and they gave me a lot of Skill Points. It was the straw that broke the camel's back for my fire magic. A window appeared with a blank avatar doing a backward-sweeping arm motion.

— Fire Upgrade: Wildfire learned! —

Getting a level three spell would have been great if the window didn't block my vision. The flying creatures hit me and Peragon hard, taking a good chunk from my Hit Points before I could even close the window. After finally clearing my vision, I didn't hesitate to drag my new fire spell into my Key Triggers to get some revenge.

I swept my arm backward to cast the spell and unleashed the wave of fire.

If it hadn't caused a hundred burnt feathers to fly into

my mouth, I might have screamed a "holy crap!" at the sheer power and spread of the fire.

The cloud of Bats burned into a cloud of ash. The Ravens caught on fire and streaked down toward the mountain. I couldn't help but let out a scream of exhilaration as I flew through the sudden heat.

My Mana was now pretty much gone, so I was forced to swerve and dodge the larger monsters that flew at me, using my Wind Blasts to clear a path so I could land. Pulling up before I hit the side of the mountain, I swooped over the snowy terrain and jumped from Peragon's back to face the remaining enemies on foot. Peragon became a Summoning Stone again, and I returned it to my items, watching the remaining monsters approach.

I had to retreat up the mountain a bit to replenish enough Mana to use my Ice Regeneration ability. Even then, my attacks only did enough to weaken them. I managed to slow down the last few with a Gravity Well, so I could execute a few more attacks, taking out the flying leopard-like creature and two remaining Ravens. Exhaling heavily, I regretted not using Gravity Well first. It certainly made finishing off the last few monsters a whole lot easier.

I turned and headed up the mountain, cold winds whipping at my robe tail. Darkness from the deep gray clouds above seemed to cover the mountain. Jagged rock stuck high up in the billowing clouds, black in the places that it wasn't covered in a layer of snow. Considering Sky Island, with its flowing waterfall, was above the Penance Mountains, I figured the temperature must rise again once a player flew past the dark clouds.

I used a Willow Bark to recover some health and then

equipped the goggles and scarf I had purchased in Lucineer. It was too bad my tolerance to the cold wasn't what it had been a week ago, for the air was biting and the sleet felt like needles on my skin. I looked up through the rain, wiping my goggles to see clearly.

As Data had said, there was a dim light above me that I now saw resonating through a large crack in the granite. I moved toward it, the wind screaming at me just like it had when climbing the glacier bridge to the stone altar, where Brock and I had fought the Ice Dragon. The déjà vu was so strong that I didn't even feel surprised when a similar Ice Dragon swooped from the dark clouds and landed above the cracked opening. The moonlight made its wings glitter, and I froze in terror.

But how? That's the boss from the Lucineer Glacier!

I didn't think it had seen me in the darkness yet. Whether it was a guardian to the entrance of the Gateway or just a combination of a Chaos Engine and some really bad luck, I had no intention of fighting the thing by myself. I didn't want to waste any items I might need in the Tertiatier dungeon—I had to ration my Willow Bark as it was. Instead, I used my dwindling Mana to increase my speed and bolted up the hill.

Approaching the perched Ice Dragon, I used some of my remaining Mana to cast Gravity Pull on it. It didn't cost as much to use as Gravity Well, which was better for fighting groups anyway.

If the Ice Dragon hadn't seen me before, it had now, its glowing eyes pointing down in my direction. It raised its head, a blue glow radiating from its mouth. As the dragon's Ice Breath rushed toward me, I raised my fist and launched a Fire Weave, shielding me from the icy blast just long enough for me to slide under it into the crack in the rock. With the very last of my Mana, I used Ice Wall to block off the entrance to the cave. This stopped the Ice Dragon from freezing the insides of the cave and me along with it, not that the insides of the cave didn't look frozen over already.

The dragon raked at the ice with its claws, but it couldn't get in. I moved further in, shivering and breathing on my hands. My mad dash hadn't stopped my fingers from going numb.

I stopped when I saw the Gateway at the end of a short tunnel, sighing in relief that I had made it.

I brought up my shared chat window and said: "You all ready?"

Everyone replied with an affirmative in their own characteristic ways, so I pulled out my Transfer Orb. Going through the menu it brought up, I selected Galrinth—our designated meeting place—and like when using a Gateway, I felt the dizzying sensation as I appeared in the Galrinth town square.

Everyone was there. At least everyone who said they would be, including another tank that I didn't think would actually show up, Sirswift himself. I shuffled over to them and saw that David was talking a lot to hide his nerves. After all, for him, Chloe, Keri, and me, this was practically a suicide mission.

"You see what I mean?" David exclaimed as he held up his new axe. "This may give me more strength, but I can really only use it for a final attack because of the amount of backlash it has on my stamina. This makes it so . . . . Oh hey, Noah!"

He looked relieved that I had come, as though he was

running out of subjects to make small talk about.

"I can't believe you got Sirswift to come with us!" Keri gushed.

"Another babysitter?" Chloe murmured, arms crossed.

"Tsh, this babysitter's going to help you stay alive," Data retorted. "Swifty knows more about this dungeon than I do."

"Good of you to join us," I said, not sure if I meant it.

He shrugged, his expression stoic. "I'm interested to see if your tactics hold up against Tertiatier monsters."

Ignoring his slight, I turned from him to Chloe and Keri, Keri beaming her usual cheerful smile at me. "Thanks for coming, both of you."

Keri shook her head. "No need to thank me. It'll be fun. I've never been in a party with enough accumulated Skill Points to get into a Tertiatier dungeon before."

"None of us have," David added with a heavy shrug.

Siena cleared her throat with an audible "ahem!"

David rolled his eyes and gestured to the other girls. "None of *us*."

"What's this place called anyway?" Siena asked.

"The Rubik's Castle; it's like a castle that's also a Rubik's Cube," Data said.

"Wow, I've heard some Tertiatier dungeons are odd, but man, a Rubik's Cube?" Chloe's voice seemed incredulous. I guess one of us had to be.

"Whoever chose this dungeon will be hoping to split us up while we're in there," Data said. "I'll explain more when we get there, but in the beginning, it will be best if we try to stick together."

"This Transfer Orb you have . . ." Sirswift directed at me. "Is it a green one or a red one?"

"Green. I've got it set up so that we can all use it to go straight to the Gateway."

"Well, I hope you don't get yourself killed in there then. You wouldn't want to lose such a valuable item." There was something disingenuous in his voice.

I remembered then what going to a Tertiatier dungeon meant for regular players. I was risking the same thing as every other time I'd taken on a fight I wasn't sure I could win, but these were new stakes for them. They could lose their items to other players. And I knew how much they valued some of those items. It made me realize what they were willing to sacrifice for me simply because I had an obsession with saving Sue. Especially David, Chloe, and Keri.

I guess we have become pretty good friends.

I didn't want to make a big thing of it, so I just said, "When I activate my Transfer Orb, select the Penance Peak's caves and you'll arrive at the Gateway."

"Alright!" David looked eager to begin. "Let's do this!"

All seven of us vanished from the Galrinth Square and appeared in the cave I had left a few minutes before. Sirswift immediately walked in the direction of the glowing Gateway. The others followed suit, and I went after them but was pulled back by Chloe.

"Noah, about the other day . . ."

This really wasn't the time, so I said, "I know, and it may seem like I'm risking a lot, and I am, but I'm here for another reason as well."

She looked down. "What reason?"

"There's something I want in there."

Someone I have to rescue.

She grinned at me, and I saw something in her face I

hadn't noticed before: passion. "Then let's go get it."

"Hello you two!" Siena called. "Stop flirting and get over here!"

"Let's go!" David called again, but I was beginning to think he was yelling out of nervousness rather than enthusiasm.

We walked over to the platform the Gateway was hovering over and selected the option to go into the Rubik's Castle Tertiatier dungeon. My heart pounded. This was it—the moment I would be able to test everything I had been through since entering Dream State. I could only pray that it was enough to keep us alive.

Chapter 24
THE TRAP

We appeared in a dark glade, standing outside the largest Rubik's Cube I'd ever seen in my life. The Gothic castle rested in a large crater at the top of the mountain. The towers, covered in brick, mortar, crenulations, and gargoyles, all shifted jerkily. Rubble crumbled from the castle as one section moved back and a giant balcony moved up to take its place. The entire middle section then twisted, revealing a doorway. The very ground beneath us shook as the castle's base pulled inward and the doorway dropped down in front of us. With the entrance now before us, it finally stopped moving.

"Whoa, that's crazy!" David called. "It doesn't even make architectural sense!"

"The Rubik's Castle . . . I can see what you mean about this place being used to separate a party," Siena said to Data, her tone serious. "But hey, no point in playing if you're not going to have fun with it!" She flicked her ponytail behind her mailed shoulder. "I'm going on ahead!"

"What? No!" Data yelled, but we could only watch as

she rushed into the castle's entrance.

"Let her go," I said. "You might as well try to stop a wolf from howling at the moon."

"Tsh, and if *you* had one of the Color Blades maybe I would be less annoyed by her rushing ahead." He sighed and turned to me. "I can only hope she takes out some of the monsters before we get stuck in different areas. Considering it's a Rubik's Cube, there will be twenty-seven rooms, so we should eventually meet up with her if we can survive long enough."

"We're wasting time," Chloe said, stalking forward. "If I'm going to die in this place, I don't plan on dragging it out."

We followed Chloe, though Sirswift's natural height allowed him to stride on ahead of her. Having the tank in front was more reassuring than a Range Niche, and I really thought Chloe should have figured that out by now.

Unlike the Penance Peaks, the wind wasn't as strong here, as though the mountain peak was the eye of a storm. This made it so the long tussocks we passed to get to the castle's main doors barely swayed.

Chloe opened the large, black doors, and we all shuffled in. The air inside smelled stale. Like a Gothic mansion after an earthquake, the castle had toppled furniture everywhere and large paintings fallen from their hooks. No monsters and no sign of Siena. We moved into the next room, a decrepit lounge filled with a broken table and chairs, its walls covered in mold and cobwebs. Before we could get to the opposite door, the entire wall shifted to the side. The door was replaced by a winding staircase leading up to a temporary second floor.

"Climb it quickly, before the walls shift again!" Data

commanded.

We ran up the stairs. I cast Speed Amp on David when I noticed him lagging behind. Bringing up the rear, he managed to use his bulk to make sure none of us were left behind. However, even though we all made it, the floor then shifted beneath us and David lost his balance.

"David!" Chloe and Keri both called in concern.

He waved his arms to regain his footing, but as the castle moved again, he fell back and tumbled down the stairs. The whole room we were in spun, and with a yell from my friend, we were down one more player.

"Crap!" Data said, pulling out his blade. "Let's see if we can re-shuffle these cards a bit."

He began cutting through one of the wooden walls of the dilapidated room we had entered. Boards splintered and broke away until there was a gap in the wall. Data moved inside and smirked as he looked through the hole, having found some method to cheat our way through portions of the dungeon.

"Ha, this should save us some time!" he said.

His pride didn't last long. As soon as we went to follow him through the wall, the floor he'd moved onto jolted and began to rise further up into the castle.

"Oh crap, no!" Data yelled, knowing right away that he had made the same mistake he had been warning everyone else about. "Stay in that hall! I'll be back soon! Swift, look after—"

His voice was cut off by a thick wall that had replaced the wooden one. My eyes narrowed as I realized why this was where they had chosen to keep Sue hostage. It was the perfect dungeon to manipulate, not only so that someone couldn't get out, but also to separate a party so they could be defeated one by one. It was a simple divide and conquer tactic.

"Come this way. There's a hall in this area." Sirswift turned to the opening leading from the stairs. "If Data tries to make a hole in the floor, there's a better chance for him to find us if we go in there."

"What about David?" Keri asked in concern.

"He's probably already dead. This is a Tertiatier dungeon, after all."

As much as I hated to admit it, he was right. *On the bright side, so long as he doesn't get killed by another player, he might not lose any items.*

I nodded and moved through the opening into the long hall. Compared to the bleak lounge below, the hall was adorned with chandeliers and spiraling candle holders on the high walls. It looked like it had once been used to host balls and other decadent occasions. I knew coming in here was a bad idea as soon as the shadows began to move. There was no light, no shifting candle or torch. The shadows moved on their own and coalesced into hissing, monstrous shapes with glowing red eyes. The castle rumbled, and I stepped back as I noticed their Hit Points, or lack thereof.

Sirswift stepped forward, drawing his long Elven Blade. "I knew something like this would happen. You three go ahead, down the hallway!"

He charged in to fight the shadow monsters but stopped as, with a jarring impact, the floor between us split apart, sinking into the basement.

"Wait!" I yelled, but Sirswift just smiled at the inevitability of us being separated.

"There's no point in trying to stick together . . ." He blocked the claw of a shadow monster and grinned back at us. "*Someone* is controlling this dungeon, moving it on purpose to separate us." He slashed out, cutting the monster in two and jumping back from the attack of another. "You might as well accept it and go to him. There's no escaping it."

But how can I win against someone who controls this entire dungeon? Has Bitcon managed to hack its code?

I wanted to ask the question, but the room was sealed shut before I could, leaving Keri, Chloe, and me alone in the darkness of the hall. The open room had been replaced from above with a stripped wall and a gaping doorway.

"I can see a hallway inside, he told us to go down it so stay close to me."

Keri moved forward with me, hands clasped in front of her. "But Sirswift—"

"There's nothing we can do about it now," Chloe finished for her, taking the words right out my mouth. "I'm eager to know who can hack into the game's template."

They followed me into the wide corridor, and I saw large braziers on either side of the room's long blue carpet. As soon as I reached the first braziers, they flared up with bright green flames, the same color as the jade of Bitcon's Color Blade. The fact that he had dropped one of the Torn Note Pieces made me think that this wasn't just a coincidence.

"I don't know for sure, but I think it might be a player called Bitcon," I said. "All Data has told me about him is that he tried to claim certain dungeons for Rare Metal farming and that, if he wanted to, he could have easily been Hero rank. Other than that, I can only guess. Come on."

Chloe came to my side as we moved down the night-blue carpet, green fire flaring up in the braziers as we passed.

"Is this guy obsessed with you or something?" she asked. "With the amount of effort being put into getting you alone, I'm beginning to think he's got a massive grudge against you."

We continued walking. "The note he left last time we fought hinted that this place or a place nearby is where my girlfriend is being kept."

"Girlfriend?" Keri asked.

I winced a little. I had tried to hint at Sue in the Grotto, but I hadn't really managed to get any actual details out. It was easier to talk about her now that she was so close.

"Yeah." I clenched my jaw at the thought. "That's why I was so determined to come here. If I can find out who this guy is, I might be able to get him to lead me to her."

"What makes you think she's even in here?" Chloe asked.

"Messages that were hidden for me in the game."

Chloe rolled her eyes. "Sounds more like wishful thinking to me."

It can't just be wishful thinking, can it?

We walked on in silence.

The braziers continued to light up one by one on either side of us, casting an eerie glow. The hallway was much longer than I had first assumed. As we reached the end of the carpet, the braziers lit ahead of us, forming a circle at the corridor's dead end. The floor then jolted, splitting behind us and rising to the third floor. I realized that the hallway didn't actually have a roof. The ceiling had just been blocked by the floor of the room above. What had been a corridor was now open to the elements, the only exit being a three-story drop where the dead end had been.

As the room rose and the roof slid away, we could see nothing but the bright stars in the night sky above us. On the bright side, the cool air wasn't as foul up here, and every detail of the room was now visible to us. This included its lack of windows and doors, the lack of a back wall, and a figure standing at the center of the circle of flickering braziers. In the moonlight, I could see that the green flames created no smoke.

The back of Bitcon's familiar black cloak faced us, tail fluttering in the freezing breeze. He turned to us and I gasped. His horned hood hid his face, but there was nothing there to cover up who was lying on the ground behind him. It was Sue, the same dark hair, the same gentle face. Only a flowing white dress covered her thin, shivering frame. Seeing her bare legs made even me feel cold.

"Sue!" I screamed. "I'll get you out of here as quick as I can!"

"Is that really her?" Chloe asked.

I watched as Sue's avatar stood up, her expression fearful, just as it had been before the car had flipped. "Yeah, that's Sue's face."

Keri shivered in the cold, but Chloe just raised an eyebrow and said, "But it doesn't make sense . . . . If she has been here the whole time, why doesn't she have a poster on the Wanted Board?"

I hesitated. "You're right! How is that even pos—"

"Noah." Sue's trembling voice stopped me mid-sentence.

My heart skipped a beat.

It's her!

"What do we do, Noah?" Chloe asked, a black knife in each hand, ready to fight.

Keri just shook her head.

I didn't know what I should do. Here I was, standing face-to-face with the girl I had thought I had killed, and all I could do was listen to her voice.

Bitcon stalked toward me, his Jade Edge flashing into his open hand. I ground my teeth. I wasn't going to let this bastard get the better of me. My time here was nearly up.

Looking over my shoulder, I caught Chloe and Keri's eyes and nodded to them. My Cursed Druid Staff appeared in my hand with a flash, and I cast a Gravity Well. A red window appeared as I attempted the arm movement.

— Program error! —

"What the . . . ? " I returned to my Key Triggers and tried accessing my items instead, but the same message appeared in my vision.

— Program error! —

"Why?"

I couldn't fathom it but, for some reason, my magic and items were both inaccessible.

The flames around us seemed to gain life then, each of them hopping from the braziers to land on the floor. They began to grow, spreading upwards in the wind and forming the shapes of people. As their avatars solidified, I recognized some of them. Two were the Wanted-ranked players from Sirswift's team who I had seen flying on mounts around Onjira. As for the rest, I recognized most of their faces from posters on the Wanted Boards . . . some of them among the highest ranked players in the game.

Events started to come together for me, and I paused. "But that means—"

"There's more than one of them?" Chloe's outraged tone seemed almost funny considering the situation.

"What do we do, Noah?" Keri asked.

"Cast some support magic on me!" I yelled.

Bitcon and Sue moved to the side of the room as the Wanted players drew toward us. They raised their arms as different weapons flashed into their hands. Bitcon had planned this ambush perfectly. My last resort was to use my Transfer Orb and get us out of there. However, as I went to access my items to activate it, I once again received the program error.

"You've got be kidding me!"

I tried again and again. Every time I used the Key Trigger for it, the program error popped up. My stats were boosted from Keri's spells, but I didn't think it would be enough without any of my spells or weapons.

They seemed to loom over us now, blocking out Bitcon's smile. His men fell upon us, swinging their weapons. I jumped back from the path of a morning star as the player wielding it was struck by Chloe's black shuriken. Keri was trying to paralyze them, but there were too many of them. It seemed the whole area had been rigged to bypass the quota of combatants for a Tertiatier dungeon, which should have been impossible. This threat was far beyond our ability to deal with.

If Keri hadn't cast Speed Amp on me beforehand, I wouldn't have been able to dodge half of their attacks.

"No! No! No!" Chloe cried out desperately as she tried to toss more knives at them, but her avatar was meant for range fighting only, not close-quarters combat.

Behind me, a Wanted player launched a fire spell. Luckily, I still had my Dragon Arm equipped so the damage was minimal.

Chloe was struck down by a warrior's axe through the red haze of the flame. I gaped as her black leathers marked the spot where she'd fallen. Keri's back was to mine, but she was a White Mage and could only support me. We were surrounded, and I was out of ideas.

"Noah, I'm going to make you Enraged, okay?" Keri whispered. "Fight with all you have!"

I don't have much to fight with without my spells!

She finished the spell just before another caster trapped her in a block of ice. Her frozen body was then shattered by a tank with a large, spiked mace, her White Rabbit Ribbon fluttering down between the shards of ice. I was alone, but I felt the spell's effect on my stats, as well as on my emotions. This must have been what the Heavies experienced when they went on a rampage, a kind of bloodlust. I equipped my Crystal Blades, ensuring Ice Regeneration was in my Key Triggers, and started hacking and stabbing.

Whoever had set this trap must have thought I'd be alone. I was locked out of my weapons, spells, items, and abilities—all but one. They must have set up a barrier for my Key Triggers that needed thoughts to activate, but Ice Regeneration only required a gesture. Each time the Crystal Blades shattered, I used the Ice Regeneration ability to summon a new set. It wasn't enough.

I struck out at a Heavy, but his Hit Points were barely fazed by my attack, and he charged me with a shield the size of a door. The impact threw me onto the carpet, and I was down to less than one third of my health. As the last one left, outnumbered and outmatched, I thought that if this were a film, now would be the time when the friends whom I had been separated from would appear to save me. However, no one could come to my rescue.

The Wanted players surrounded me again. Even as they blocked my vision of the room, I couldn't help but wonder what I had done to deserve this. I couldn't fathom anything I had done that was so bad that someone would have set up something like this. The Heavy lifted his mace to finish me off.

"Stop!" a familiar voice yelled.

The Heavy paused and lowered his weapon. An avatar that looked like an old wizard pulled him aside as others followed suit, creating a gap for Bitcon to walk into. Behind them, the figure of Sue lying on the floor suddenly flickered and then disappeared from the room. I choked on my breath, looking up to see Bitcon looming over me. I could see he was smiling at me under his hood.

Seeing that smile, it hit me, and I suddenly understood why I had recognized him the first time we fought. I had thought he was someone I'd met before. I had assumed from the points under his hood that his avatar had horns. I now realized that I only recognized his grin from seeing his Wanted poster, and what I thought were horns weren't horns at all, but pointed Elven ears.

The best player in the Dream State . . .

I ground my teeth. "*Swifty*, what have you done with Sue?"

"Oh, she's the last thing you should be worrying about," he said as he crouched down in front of me and removed his hood. "And please, do call me Bitcon."

Chapter 25

FAULT

"I see your whole team is in on this," I said, looking around at the familiar faces.

"Not just them. Remember who I work for." Bitcon stood up, gesturing to the room. "The entire Wona Company has been manipulating the Dream State's template, just to get you to come to this place."

My mind was trying to get around how they had managed to lure me here. It was the Torn Note Pieces that had drawn me to this dungeon, but how could they have made sure that I received them? Were they tracking me everywhere I went in the game? That didn't seem likely. Each dungeon I had found the items in were dungeons I had mentioned while using their messaging system. Maybe that was their method? I was also one of their clients so, of course, they knew about Sue and my accident. They had used all this against me, but to what end?

I couldn't get Sue's flickering image out of my head. I had to get out of here alive so I could figure out where Bitcon had sent her.

"Why me?" I asked. "Why all this when I'm so close to waking up?"

"Because you have something they want." His Jade Edge vanished from his hand, and he pointed down at me. "And the only way to get it is to kill you in this place. Every Dream State item is their property, and they want that one back."

"An item?" Confusion tore through me like a storm. "The Wona Company, a billion-dollar industry, manipulated their entire game, just to get an item . . . from *me?*"

Bitcon inclined his head. "A very valuable item, stolen from the company a while back and given to you by a close friend of yours."

I searched my memory, thinking of the people who had given me items in the past. "Datalent?"

"This is not a guessing game, Noah. The only reason you're still alive is because you've somehow managed to trick real players into carrying you through the game. You haven't earned any of your rankings. And I can't let that stand. So either you give me that valuable item right now and admit defeat, or we prove once and for all whether or not you're good enough for a Tertatier dungeon."

His grin widened, and he stood, looking down at me contemptuously. He then turned and walked away as though offering me to his goons. Again, my mind raced. Thinking back on his words and what Data had told me when I had first met him, a sudden idea struck me.

He's an elitist! He needs everyone to know how good he is!

"Don't you think that's a little hypocritical coming from you?" I asked.

He stopped, looking at me over his shoulder. "I'm sorry?"

"You said my rankings are unearned, but as far as I'm

concerned, you had nothing to do with bringing me down—your team did that for you." I shook my head derisively "But if you were to fight me one-on-one, I don't think you could beat me."

"Ha, you're joking," he said.

Despite trying to play this off, Bitcon's eyes were wide, and I knew I had him.

"Honestly, I was always confused why people thought you were the best player in the game." I shrugged. "Sure, you have the highest Survival Record, but look at your team! For Pete's sake, anyone could last that long with these kinds of players to back them up!"

"What? You think my team is the reason I'm the best?" He laughed, but it sounded forced. "The only reason these guys even have Wanted ranks is because I'm in *their* team! But heck, if that's what you think . . ."

His Jade Edge flashed back into his hand, and he advanced on me.

One of Bitcon's teammates, the dark-skinned Warrior, walked up to him. "I don't think you should, Swifty. He's just trying to get you to—"

"Do you want to go back to working in a convenience store, huh?" Bitcon lashed out at him. "The only reason you're getting paid to play games is because my uncle is the CEO of Wona!"

The one that looked like an old wizard shifted to Bitcon's side and whispered, "Remember what Malcolm told you. I don't think he would be happy with you forgetting about the job he gave you just so you can stroke your ego."

Bitcon spread his hands. "He's going to die either way, so what's the difference? Just stay out of this."

"I can't use my items or spells," I interjected. "It wouldn't be fair if I fought you without them. What is a Spellcaster without magic and items?"

"Ah!" Bitcon's brow raised and he waved a finger in my face. "Very clever, Noah! That's why you've survived for so long. But don't think I don't see through your plan. You want me to free up your items so you can escape with your Transfer Orb, am I right?"

The shoulders of the Spellcaster who had been reprimanding him seemed to relax. Bitcon was dead right, but I wasn't about to give that away.

"I'm not going anywhere without Sue," I lied.

"Ha, I am right! I can tell from your pulse. We are given direct feed to your vitals through the Dream Engine. We can measure whenever you're getting . . . excited." Bitcon laughed and nodded. "But sure, why not? I'll make this a fair fight."

"What!" the old wizard exclaimed.

I was surprised too. He knew what I was going to do if he freed up my Key Triggers.

"Don't do it," the dark Warrior called.

"You'll risk everything if he escapes!" The old wizard growled. "Just kill him now!"

Bitcon turned his confident grin on me. "He won't try to escape."

"And how do you know that?" The Spellcaster was starting to sound agitated.

By this point in the conversation, I was honestly curious about this myself.

"Because I know he'll want to remain to fight me," Bitcon said, as though glad his teammate had asked. "He won't be able to help himself."

Shows what he knows.

"What gives you that idea?" I asked. The words seemed to come spilling out of my mouth unbidden.

Bitcon spread his hands to his sides. "Because I was the driver who followed you onto the highway, and the truck driver who crashed into your car was this guy here!" He pointed to the Wanted-ranked Heavy wielding the mace, a big, dumb grin on his barbarian face. "You're in here because of us."

That can't be true!

I recalled the crash, how someone had been riding my tail onto the highway, beeping his horn, trying to make me go faster . . . making sure I was in the right place for the truck to crash into me.

"But I was under the influence of DSD!" I cried. "It was my fault!"

"Come now, Noah. You were at a set of red lights on the highway, over a dozen yards apart!" Bitcon pointed to his friend. "Do you really think that he couldn't have stopped if he wanted to? He crashed into you because Wona paid him to! Whereas me, I would have done it for free! You should have warned your girlfriend not to play with fire. That loudmouth put a good number of powerful people on edge when she wrote that petition."

He had been right. When it came to Sue, it turned out I really was that predictable. I rose to my feet, a sudden rage burning inside of me. *He won't get away with this!*

"No, Swifty, don't!" called the old wizard.

Access to my items and magic was restored immediately. Maybe the Enrage spell was still affecting my emotions because instead of what I knew I should have done, I selected not my Transfer Orb, but my staff. I had enough Mana that I could use both Speed Amp on myself and Gravity Well on Bitcon.

I used neither. Wildfire raged from my staff and turned the room into a furnace, not to hurt him but to blind him. With fire filling the room, I summoned two Crystal Blades and struck out at where I had seen him standing. Where he no longer was. As my first blade slashed nothing but flame, I spun and ducked as Bitcon's Jade Edge slashed over me. As I attempted to stab at him, a wall of ice shot up from the floor between us.

His use of magic reminded me of his fight with Data in the Penance Mines, how he had blown up a wall of earth with a Fire Weave. I realized he was going to use the same tactic. Before he could, I recalled my staff and directed a Wind Blast into the explosion, which blew the blast of ice away from me. He came on, Jade Edge gleaming. My own blades flashed into my hands, and I fought. Slashing and stabbing, ducking and dodging, but I wasn't the only one who had learned from the last time we had fought.

As fragile as my swords were, Bitcon knew that they were no threat against his Color Blade, and he carved his way through my defenses as shards of ice fell to the carpet. Only when no more weapons appeared in my hands did I realize my Mana had completely run out. Panicking, I retreated as he swung at me. From out of nowhere, a glowing arrow hit my ankle. It didn't take many Hit Points, but I stumbled back from the pain, tripped over one of the braziers, and went to lean against the stone wall. A stone wall that wasn't there.

Oh crap!

When the room at the end of the hall had risen to the top floor, locking us in, the back wall had been replaced with nothing but open air . . . open air I was now falling out into. My stomach rose into my mouth as I plummeted. Despite how high the ceiling of each room was, I wouldn't have time to summon Peragon.

Before I could even think, I landed on something cold and hard, but which wasn't the ground.

"Got you! Oh man! Not to brag or anything, but that was perfect timing!"

I was lying across the scaly back of a giant monster made of ice, a dragon to be exact, and straddling it in front of me, bow in hand, was the last person I had expected to save me.

"Brock?"

He still had his cheesy grin, even in a situation like this.

"Hold on, Noah, I'm getting you out of here!"

My first reaction when seeing him riding the same monster that had attacked me at the Gateway: *Wait, you can get the Ice Dragon as a mount?*

My second reaction as a blue glow filled the Ice Dragon's eyes and mouth: *Hang on, mounts can use attacks?*

My last reaction as the Ice Breath attack filled the room I had just fallen from: *Oh no, Sue's in that room!*

"No, Sue! Brock, stop!" I screamed as he steadied me to keep me from falling off. "She might still be in there somewhere!"

"Don't you get it yet?" Brock yelled as we began to rise into the cold night. "That wasn't really her! Wona altered an Illusion spell to make it look like anyone they have a photo of, including Sue!"

"No, it had to be her! I heard her voice!"

"It was artificial, Noah! They must have used the videos of her from her petition's website to synthesize a recording that sounded like her! She was bait for their trap, and you took it, hook, line, and sinker!"

A trap, just like Data said. It turned out I did have something worth stealing after all. Was it really possible?

I recalled her trembling voice. At first, I'd thought she sounded that way because she was cold. Only now did I realize how fake it had sounded, not to mention how she had simply flickered off like a television with a bad signal. Nausea came over me as all of my hope and wishful thinking collapsed in on itself.

If Sue wasn't really here, if her mind wasn't really trapped somewhere in the game, then she really was dead. There was no way to save the small part of her that I'd hoped remained in here. I had lost her all over again. The familiar cold panic I'd felt while talking to my mother returned. Yet I had gone through this grief before, and I knew how to control it. Taking a deep breath in, I pushed the grief down, burying it deep beneath the soil of everything else I had learned today and stomping down the dirt with a fierce determination to move forward. I could exhume it when I was out of this mess, but as for right now, I had to stay alive.

Chapter 26

THE BEAUTY OF HINDSIGHT

Rising into the dark sky, Brock pulled out a green Transfer Orb, and in a flash of light, we vanished from the air above the Rubik's Castle. We appeared in a Basetier city that I'd never been to before, and a scroll unrolled over my vision to tell me that we had arrived in New Calandor. The place looked like a colonial city, maybe eighteenth-century America or Victorian Europe.

Brock's Ice Dragon landed on the dark brick road, blocking the traffic of wagons and coaches driven by foppish-looking NPCs.

I was still stunned by the loss of Sue. "Where are we?"

Brock returned the Ice Dragon to a white Summoning Stone. "Okay, they shouldn't be able to follow us here right away. Not all of them, anyhow. This city is an expansion only those who have cleared a Tertiatier dungeon can access. It doesn't appear on your maps list unless you have survived for at least an hour in one. That's probably why you haven't heard of it until now."

"You said that only people who've survived a Tertiatier dungeon can come here?"

"That's right."

"And it's safe to assume that Bitcon's team are among those who have?"

"I get your point. I'll explain quickly. There's a lot you need to know." He moved down another brick road, beckoning me to follow him. "Let's find a place to sit down. There's nothing like an explanation of why you nearly died to help you get over the fact that you nearly died."

I nodded as we made our way past NPC men in tuxedos and women wearing lace over tight corsets and carrying frilly umbrellas. The scent of perfume pervaded the air from both the women and the men. I didn't know if it was just the NPCs in this part of the city that dressed in such an elegant fashion or if the players were encouraged to as well. Either way, in my robes, I stood out in the crowd.

The swirling gray clouds in the overcast sky suggested the coming of the storm that I had seen south of the city, much like the wet weather that England was known for.

"Wait, is this the city blocked off by that lightning storm north of Onjira?"

"That's the one. It's called the Storm Wall." Brock raised his brow. "Neat, huh?"

It certainly answers my questions about that wall of bad weather.

All around us were massive buildings of the Victorian architecture carved from large sandy-white stone. We entered one of the larger buildings, a restaurant, and I saw right away why access to this area was only given to those who had survived Tertiatier. It was the most civilized place I had seen in Basetier, and I could only guess what the dungeons were like here.

Brock chose one of the many small tables to sit down at. A string quartet played to one side of us, and a crystal chandelier hung above our heads. The place smelled like wood smoke. Around us, I heard the murmur of other players and the robotic questions of the NPC waitresses. I shifted uneasily in the plush seat, and Brock waved at a passing NPC waitress in a maid outfit. He whispered something to her when she came over, and then she moved off.

"Okay, talk. Why haven't you been replying to my messages?" I asked, but then I shook my head as a more important question took priority in my mind. "Why is the Wona Company after me?"

Brock's face became suddenly serious. "First off, I'm sorry for not replying. They blocked my messaging after Lucineer. Now tell me, do you still have the Transfer Orb?"

"Yeah, why?"

Brock sighed in relief. He curled his fingers in a gesture for me to take it out. "Let me show you."

I accessed my items and brought out the green Transfer Orb. He took it, and his gaze went distant as he looked at his menu for a moment. A window with a video feed appeared in my vision. The image was focused on a reclining chair in a wide, empty room. A young Asian man wearing a Dream Engine helmet sat in the chair. The thing covered his head from his eyes to the top of his spine, and he had intravenous tubes in his arms.

"It should be playing now," Brock said.

I nodded. “I see it. What is this?”

“Just watch.”

Nothing happened for a moment, but then what was silence became the sound of choking. The young man started shaking. Then the shaking became convulsions. Foam and vomit began to spill out of his mouth.

A man wearing a nurse’s mask ran in and rolled him on his side, but after a minute of sharp shakes, the young man became still. The nurse yanked off his helmet and tried to resuscitate him. After another minute, the nurse stopped, unsuccessful.

Sickened by what I had just seen, I shook my head, covering my mouth. “What the hell?”

“He died,” Brock said. “And there are six other videos on there that are just like that. It’s evidence of the drug overdoses the DSD beta testers had.” Brock passed the orb back to me. “Wona covered it up and made everyone sign confidentiality agreements. I refused and made a copy of the videos before I was fired. They were forced to forge my signature. After that they raided my house. I’d already fled and wiped my hard drive. Those are the only copies of the videos left.”

Everything suddenly made sense. “So, what you told Sue and me . . . that was true?”

He returned the orb to my inventory. “And by telling you, I dragged you and Sue into this mess. Sue mentioned that I was sending her the videos on her online petition. That must have been how they found out about the two of you. To cover it up entirely, they tried to have you both killed.”

“Wait, Sue said you sent the videos to her on a flash drive. Would they still be on her computer?”

Brock shook his head. “They claimed the drive and her

computer, yours too. I tried to get my hands on them first after you told me what happened, but I was too late." He smirked. "Nearly got caught that time. As I said, what's on the orb are the last copies."

I shook my head in disbelief. It was too much to process all at once. For now, I just had to make sure I survived long enough to be woken up and tell everyone what I knew. So long as I was in this game, I was under their power. I was going to need protection. Yet I didn't know who I could trust.

My mother had mentioned getting help from the Wona Company right after the accident. Maybe they had convinced her to buy Datalent's service so he could keep an eye on me and distract me from what I had heard.

Does that mean Data is in on all of this as well?

"Why did Bitcon attack Data in the Penance Mines if they were working together?"

"They weren't. Datalent, the tool, has no idea of any of this. Bitcon is the boss of a secret division of Wona. His uncle is the CEO of Wona, so just think of Bitcon's team as Wona's in-game hitmen that Bitcon runs like a dictator. Data, on the other hand, really is just an ignorant guide. Now that everything is out in the open, Bitcon will be coming after us, and we'll have to be smart to find a way to beat him."

The maid returned and placed two drinks on the table in front of us. Above each one was a glowing upward-pointing arrow with the word "Mana" underneath it. Brock gulped his down and then gestured to mine. I drank the hot liquid and watched as my Mana gauge was refilled.

"Heck, Bitcon was probably relying on Data to protect you until you could get to a Tertiatier dungeon anyway,"

Brock continued. "Now you're probably wondering why I gave you the Transfer Orb in the first place."

"I figure it's because they were tracking you and you were afraid of the implications with your signature on their agreement? No one's going to roll out the red carpet for a whistleblower trying to destroy their favorite game's manufacturer."

Brock tilted his head. "That too, but it was more to buy time than anything else. I knew they wouldn't be able to get the evidence off you until you gained enough Skill Points to get to Tertiatier. I'm actually impressed they managed to lure you there so quickly, but I didn't expect them to use Sue as bait. I thought they'd want to stay as far away from her as possible after what they did. But I shouldn't be surprised how little they value human life. After I saw your top Survival Record in the Druids' Keep, I figured something was up. I used the player tracking software from my time working for Wona to find out which dungeon you were trying to get to . . . and the rest is history."

This must have been the same software that Data and Siena used to know my location. "So, I was your insurance in case they caught you when you tried to get the flash drive back?"

Brock nodded. "Yes, but now that you know they instigated the crash that killed Sue, I bet you're glad you've kept safe the evidence that might put them away, right?"

"You're damn right." I gritted my teeth. "Bitcon's going to wish he didn't let that slip. He's confessed, there's motive—thanks to this orb—and . . . wait . . . as an admin, couldn't Bitcon just delete the item from my inventory or just check all the Transfer Orbs in the game? Surely, that would be easier than hunting me down."

Brock nodded. "That's true, although I figure that the Dream Engine the hospital put on you limited the amount of data that could be transferred so that no one could interfere with your connection to the Dream State. This would have prevented them from being able to get at the one you had. Either that or he hasn't been granted permission for that, or he just didn't know what the item code was; I honestly have no idea."

I shook my head, doubtful any of these theories was the actual reason. After all, games worked on code. Sure, there were a few Transfer Orbs in the Dream State, but it wouldn't have taken their programmers that long to find and delete the one containing the video. There had to be another reason. That Bitcon had instead lured me into a dungeon was baffling. Perhaps there was more behind all this that even Brock didn't know.

I ground my teeth. "You know, I could have avoided going to Tertiatier if I'd known about all this sooner."

"I did tell you to avoid it." Brock shrugged. "I've been in hiding for months now, and Wona is still searching for me. The only reason they haven't been able to find me in here is because I know how their tracking software works and how to make my avatar invisible to it. If I try to go to the police with evidence, they'll grab me before I can even step through the door, and after they deleted my accounts, I couldn't email the videos myself. You need to find a way to get them out there once you wake up."

"And in the meantime?"

Brock stuck out his bottom lip. "Try not to die."

"Easier said than done," I said, rolling my eyes.

"We should move on." He got up from his chair and paid the Moola for the drinks. "Besides those working for Wona, there won't be many players in Basetier trying to kill you because they won't get anything out of it. Even so, it's still logical to have safety in numbers. I suggest you get in contact with everyone who was willing to go to the Tertiatier dungeon wit—"

There was the sound of an explosion from outside, the wind from the impact whooshing in from the street, and I could hear gasps from players and NPCs alike. I turned and saw through the windows what I had been expecting to jump out from every dark corner since we had escaped the Rubik's Castle. Bitcon's team had arrived in New Calandor.

"I will after we get out of here!" I called back.

Chapter 27

FIGHT OR FLIGHT

I watched as a few of the avatars I recognized from the ambush jumped down from their various mounts and began searching the street. They weren't being too discreet about it. I could hear smashing windows and spells being launched in what was supposed to be a combat-free zone.

"I think your idea to come to this place might have just turned out of our favor."

Brock smirked. "Look on the bright side, everyone here is just as tough as me and might be able to pick off some of the weaker ones for us. That'll give us some time."

Ha, and I thought I was guilty of wishful thinking.

As though just to prove me wrong, other players began firing spells back, a tank crashing through a wall in an adjacent building to charge at them. I laughed at the chaos we had caused. The building shook as debris fell around us. Dust rained from the ceiling from each loud explosion and the attacks from their mounts. We heard screams as we covered our heads with our arms and moved between the tables toward a back exit.

Coming out onto another street, I brought out my Transfer Orb with one hand and held my Summoning Stone in the other. "Get out your stone! We'll be airborne when we reappear!"

"Sky Island?" he asked.

I nodded, and as soon as I selected the setting, we vanished from New Calandor and were falling through the air. Except for the few flying monsters soaring around in the distance and the massive island floating alongside us, the blue sky was mostly empty. In Basetier, Sky Island had the freest space to move in without being harassed by monsters, and boy, we really needed to fly. The wind whipped in our faces as we fell. I was glad we both had our Summoning Stones in hand.

Three mounts appeared in the sky. I recognized them from New Calandor: the dark-skinned Spellcaster on a Griffin and the redheaded Range Niche on his Black Dragon. Accompanying them was a blonde Warrior riding a massive bat. The uneasiness I'd felt when I'd seen them outside Onjira now made sense. They had been keeping an eye on me even then.

Brock summoned his Ice Dragon and began firing arrows at the oncoming mounts. It was three against one, however, and without my help, he wouldn't last long. I positioned my Summoning Stone below me and felt Peragon solidify between my legs. We pulled up, swooping out from the island cliff face just in time to dodge a bolt of lightning the Spellcaster had cast. I pulled back into the sky and charged at him. His Griffin was smaller but quicker than Peragon. I managed to dodge a swipe of its claws that ended up tearing a gash in my mount's leg.

I winced. *At least it wasn't a wing.*

That gave me an idea. As I spun to face another assault by the Spellcaster, I launched an Ice Coffin at the Griffin's left wing. It hit, and the Griffin nosedived, plunging its rider through the clouds below.

That was surprisingly easy.

Above me, Brock was going head-to-head against another mounted player. Being a Range Niche gave Brock a distinct advantage. The bat-riding Warrior he had been fighting fell away from him, covered in arrows. Unfortunately, the last of our pursuers was also a Range Niche, the redhead on the Black Dragon.

He and Brock circled each other, firing arrows. As I rose to join them, an arrow bounced off the Ice Dragon's armor-like scales, and Brock's own arrow was blown away by the Black Dragon's flapping wings.

Brock used his dragon's Ice Breath attack. As the Black Dragon went to dodge it, I cast a Lightning Strike at the rider. Although the spell didn't do much against him, it got his attention long enough for Brock to land a clean shot. It must have been a specialty arrow with paralytic properties, for the redhead fell stiffly from his mount.

With the Black Dragon and its rider defeated, I thought we were finally home free. However, as we drew together, I noticed in alarm the grim expression on Brock's face.

"Crap!" he yelled. "I didn't think!"

"What?"

"Wona uses the same tracking software I used to locate you. The Dream State is a big world and sometimes players can get lost in the crowd, but whenever we use a Transfer Orb, it creates a temporary Gateway that acts like a beacon for them to follow. Even if you're invisible to their tracking like I am, by timing the Gateway's creation, they can easily use it to pinpoint our location."

The first time Bitcon had attacked me personally was just after I had used the Transfer Orb to take my friends from the Goblin Dungeon to Yarburn. That's how he knew where I was. Considering how rare they were, using the orb must have confirmed to Wona that Brock had given it to me when we had met in Lucineer.

If only there was a way to . . .

An idea then struck me, and I looked down on the Penance Mountain range below us. "I should discard the orb."

"Are you kidding?" Brock asked.

"Think about it. As long as one of us has the orb, they'll continue hunting us, right? But if they don't know we don't have it, we can keep it safe even if we die." I gritted my teeth. "It's risky, I admit, but if I keep the orb, they'll either find a way to force me into a Tertiatier dungeon to steal it or resort to killing me. But if you *pretend* to have it, you can lure them away without uncovering the orb's true whereabouts. In the meantime, I can get a friend, someone they won't suspect, to go pick it up without Wona ever finding out."

Brock shook his head but then said, "I don't like it, but at the moment, it's the best plan we have."

I went into my inventory and selected the Discard option when focusing on the Transfer Orb. We both watched our last hope to avenge Sue drop and vanish into the mountains.

"Okay, now what?" Brock asked.

"Well, you did say a player can get lost in a crowd. Galrinth is always crowded so maybe we should hea—"

There was a flash in the sky above us. Bitcon and several

of his teammates came into view all at once.

I gasped. We were badly outnumbered and outmatched. With over half a dozen Wanted-ranked players facing our way, their silence was more intimidating than any words they might have spoken.

Brock seemed to be as stunned as I was, for he remained silent and still. Yet he could use his Transfer Orb and escape if he wanted to. Because of my *genius* idea to get rid of the evidence in the mountains, I couldn't.

Astride his giant serpent, Bitcon's gaze shifted to one of his teammates. "Cast Toxin on Noah, now," he ordered.

At his command, the Spellcaster who resembled an old wizard pointed his gnarled, wooden staff at me, and a green glow flew into my chest. I felt nothing, but my health visibly started to diminish. It was similar to being bitten by an Arachnid in Widows' Forest.

Bitcon caught my panicked expression and grinned. "If you don't want to die, you're going to do exactly what I say."

I watched my life slip away. "What was that?"

"A level three poison spell of which only a second-level antidote spell or certain rare items can cure. So . . ." He gestured to my Hit Points. "Unless you want to watch your life slowly slip down to nothing, you're going to give me that orb."

"But if I die you'll lose the evidence as well! If I regain consciousness then—"

"If you had just accepted your fate, we would have simply taken the Transfer Orb in Tertiatier." Bitcon shrugged. "Who knows, maybe, if you came out of your coma, you could've regained consciousness with nothing to worry about. But you had to fight it! Now that you know so much, luring you to a Tertiatier dungeon is out of the question, and as you said yourself, very soon you'll be recovered enough to wake up. We can't let that happen."

I ground my teeth as my health bar reached its halfway point. "What do you mean nothing to worry about?"

"Wona has no reason to pursue you without the orb. Once we had it, we could have left you alone."

"That might be true, but I still would have pursued you. It's your fault Sue is dead, and I would've continued this fight to the bitter end as soon as my eyes opened!"

"You only have one chance to get out of this, Noah. Give us the orb."

"I don't have it anymore."

"You're lying!"

"He's not!" Brock called. "Go on, check his inventory. I know you can!"

Bitcon's eyes widened in anger. "Where is it? Tell me!"

"I have it! He gave it to me in New Calandor!"

I looked to Brock in confusion. Did Brock really think that lying about the orb would get us out of this now? He knew I didn't have a Transfer Orb anymore; I couldn't use it to escape. Even then, my Hit Points would hit zero in a matter of seconds. I was going to die. Just hours away from finally being able to wake up, I was going to be sent into a coma. I hoped for a moment that maybe my body was recovered enough that I'd be okay. But I knew that was wishful thinking. If that were true, they would have woken me up already.

Bitcon scowled. "You've made a big mistake."

As my Hit Points dropped into the red zone, I couldn't help but agree. Despite this, Brock smirked and flew closer to me. I didn't understand why he hadn't left already. He should've been pretending to try and escape with the orb to lead them off the scent of its real location.

Does he think he can save me? What's he got up his sleeve?

"What?" Brock asked, bringing out *his* Transfer Orb from his inventory as though offering it to them. "Do you want this?"

"Hand it over now!" Bitcon yelled.

"Cast the antidote spell and I will."

"Alright then." Bitcon caught his wizard's gaze again. "As soon as he passes it over, cure Noah." He turned back to us and spread his arms. "Alright?"

Brock threw the green orb through the air toward them. I felt panic hit me like a sudden punch to the gut. That was it, as soon as he caught it, Brock's bluff would be revealed. Fortunately, the wizard kept his word and cast his spell to stop my health from plummeting. I barely had a tenth of it left.

"What are you doing?" I hissed at Brock.

Brock gave me a knowing grin and whispered, "I used an Illusion Arrow. Dismiss your mount now!"

This confused me, but as soon as Bitcon caught the orb, we both used the Key Trigger to dismiss our mounts and drop from the sky. As we fell, I looked up just in time to see the orb change color from green to red in Bitcon's outstretched hand. Bitcon's victorious grin fell, and it suddenly dawned on me.

Brock didn't pass them a Transfer Orb, but a disguised Kamikaze Orb!

The explosion ripped through the air, engulfing Bitcon's entire party in flame. The impact of the blast was immense, just like the one in the Penance Mines had been. Even though we had fallen a good distance, the shock wave was still enough to increase the speed of our fall. I screamed, seeing my health take yet another hit from the impact. I quickly used a Willow Bark item, stopping it just before it reached the one percent mark.

Another close call! How am I not dead yet?

We fell below Sky Island and through the clouds. I could see the Penance Mountains coming up to meet us. Brock reappeared and maneuvered down to fall beside me, grinning from the rush as we continued to plummet. He gestured to the Summoning Stone in his hand, signaling for me to bring out my own, his words inaudible through the wind whistling in my ears. We both summoned our mounts and leveled out from our dives.

"Woohoo!" Brock screamed, but whether from the adrenaline of the fall or the success of his plan, I couldn't tell.

I felt a bit like whooping myself. The evidence was safely hidden, the people responsible for Sue's death had just been blown up, and I was going to live long enough to get out of this game. For the first time since I had woken up inside this game, I was finally in control. The constant weight of falling into a coma seemed to lift off my shoulders. Now I just needed to lie low long enough to wake up.

Chapter 28
REALITY

We flew under the clouds into the clear skies over Galrinth. I opened up my contacts again and began reading my teammates' urgent messages to me. There were so many of them that I was glad I had turned off my message alerts before entering the Rubik's Castle so they wouldn't distract me. I figured the first thing I should tell them all was the one thing I was the most surprised of myself.

"I'm still alive."

"If we don't use a Transfer Orb or a Gateway," Brock mused, "they won't be able to tell our positions, so this will be our best chance to hide ourselves and regroup."

I nodded.

"They don't know where we dropped it, but we don't know exactly where it is either," I said. "We'll need to find it before anyone else does. Transfer Orbs are rare items, so you can bet that anyone who comes across it will claim it."

"Well, hopefully the next time I see you, I'll be able to hand it to you myself so you can send the evidence in to the police."

I nodded. "Until then, good luck."

Brock spun on his Ice Dragon and made to fly off.

Before he could, I called, "Brock, did you get your Ice Dragon to try and stop me from reaching the Penance Peaks Gateway?"

He looked over his shoulder with his usual cheesy smile. "That's the one thing Bitcon had right; fear is a good motivator, but it seems that your determination was stronger. That's something I respect about you, Noah."

I shook my head, baffled at the amount of trouble he had gotten me into. "You'll really have to pay me back for this one day."

"How about putting away Sue's killers?"

I nodded solemnly. "That'll do it."

Brock smirked and flew off.

I dropped down into the outskirts of Galrinth, landing on the grass outside the city walls. As I had arranged with some cryptic messages, the team that had gone with me to the Rubik's Castle was waiting for me next to the moat that went around the city walls, minus Sirswift of course. When I saw Data was with them, I couldn't help but feel lucky that Brock and I had separated before we met up, remembering the animosity between them.

I dismounted and walked up to them.

"I'm so sorry, there was nothing else I could have done," Keri said, not looking me in the eyes.

"I still can't figure out how you survived, Noah," Chloe said, shaking her head.

Siena gave me a more skeptical stare. "I would like to know that as well."

At least they don't sound too upset about the items they lost.

"It's fine." I returned Peragon to its Summoning Stone. "*I'm* fine."

I turned to Data, who was looking as confused as the rest of them after what I guessed Chloe and Keri had told them.

"Everyone, listen up. The crash that paralyzed me and killed my girlfriend was instigated by the Wona Company."

Keri gasped, both Chloe and Siena's eyes widened, Data's brow furrowed, and David stammered in confusion.

"Wait, so it wasn't the DSD?" David asked.

I nodded. "Bitcon and his teammate planned the crash. He admitted it to me himself."

Data seemed to take offense to this. "Tsh, Bitcon isn't a Wona employee."

"He is, under a secret division used for more unsavory jobs. Sue and I found out what the company was hiding, and they tried to have us killed in order to silence us."

"Go on," Siena said, her curiosity getting the better of her.

"During the testing stages of the Dream Engine, several beta testers died from DSD overdoses." Data looked like he was about to deny this. I caught his eye. "I saw a video of it myself."

"Show it to me!"

"The videos are encoded into a Transfer Orb that Brock gave me. That's why I was lured into a Tertiatier dungeon. They wanted to kill me there and steal the item with the evidence on it." I looked around to see they were still listening intently. "Before they could, Brock showed up and helped me to escape. We got the evidence out of their reach, but I had to leave it behind somewhere in the Penance Mountains."

Siena smiled. "It sounds like you've set up quite a treasure hunt for us."

I tilted my head. "You could look at it that way. I dropped it from the air north of Sky Island. Wherever it landed, that's where the evidence is. At the moment, Brock is searching for it by himself, but he could use our help. So, who's with me?"

Silence fell after I finished my little speech. I felt a sudden anxiety pull in my chest as I thought of the heavy burden I would be leaving my friends with. I then realized how much I trusted each of them to see this through.

David slowly raised his hand.

Chloe shook her head and forced his hand down again. "We're with you, Noah," she said, gesturing to the three in her team.

Siena brushed back her ponytail and grinned. "Seriously, Noah, you pretty much challenged me to find this thing, and when have I ever turned down a challenge?"

The five of us turned to Data, who was looking unsure.

"Swifty . . . he was Bitcon, wasn't he?" he asked, although it seemed obvious since he was the only one who hadn't rejoined our group. "That's why he was so interested in your Transfer Orb."

"Yeah . . . so are you in?"

He grimaced and turned away. "Tsh, you're asking me to go against my employers and an old friend for the sake of someone who I don't trust, nor get along with."

"Don't you think it was suspicious that Brock got fired just after you were all forced to sign a confidentiality agreement?" I asked.

His eyes narrowed. "How did you . . . ? No, it doesn't matter. I will help you find this orb, but only because finding it will help clear Wona's name."

He turned to walk through Galrinth.

"What will you do when you see that the videos exist for yourself?" I called to him.

"I'll quit." Although I couldn't see his expression, his voice sounded amused.

He vanished into the city.

"I think it's time I finally caught up with Brock as well. You say he'll be in the Penance Mountains?" David began to move in the direction of the hazy peaks in the distance. "Alright, looks like we've got some climbing to do."

"Ha, now we're talking!" Siena said as she followed in behind him.

Inspired by Siena's enthusiasm, Chloe and Keri went to follow them.

I checked my menu's clock and saw that it had been several hours since I had last spoken with my mother, which meant I might be able to wake up any minute now. Either way, I decided I should say something to the girls before that time came.

"Hey, uh . . . Keri, Chloe." They turned to me. "Soon I'll be able to wake up, and I'm not going to be coming into this game for a while. I'll probably have to go through all kinds of physiotherapy, just so I can walk again. But I will return"—I wouldn't stop until I had evidence to put away Wona—"and when I do, I'll want to play with you two again."

Chloe smirked and crossed her arms. "Of course you will. We'll have to wait and see how generous we feel at the time, though."

Keri gave me a puzzled glance and turned with Chloe, hands clasped behind her.

I went to follow them, but then a window popped up

in my vision, showing a message alert. It was my mother. I brought it up, but instead of a video feed only text appeared.

"Noah, it's time. Your DSD levels are low enough that the doctor thinks it's safe to induce the waking stimuli. Are you ready to wake up?"

Already?

I said, "I'm ready," and then shifted my gaze from the window to the four avatars walking ahead of me, dedicated to searching the mountains to find the Transfer Orb with Brock's evidence—to help me.

"Everyone!" They all turned back to look at me, confused expressions stamped on their faces when they saw that I had stopped walking. "I'll be back soon, I promise."

The only response I heard was Keri calling my name.

I said, "Do it."

In an instant, darkness was pulled over my eyes. I could no longer hear the crowd of Galrinth or whatever Keri had been trying to say. The ground was gone, as were my robes. There was nothing but the darkness.

A sudden intrusion of light pierced my vision. It was the light of the real world beneath the rim of a Dream Engine helmet.

Words glowed brightly on the inside of it:

— NotThatNoah logged out —

If you loved *Stuck in the Game*,
check out War of Kings and Monsters
by Christopher Keene!

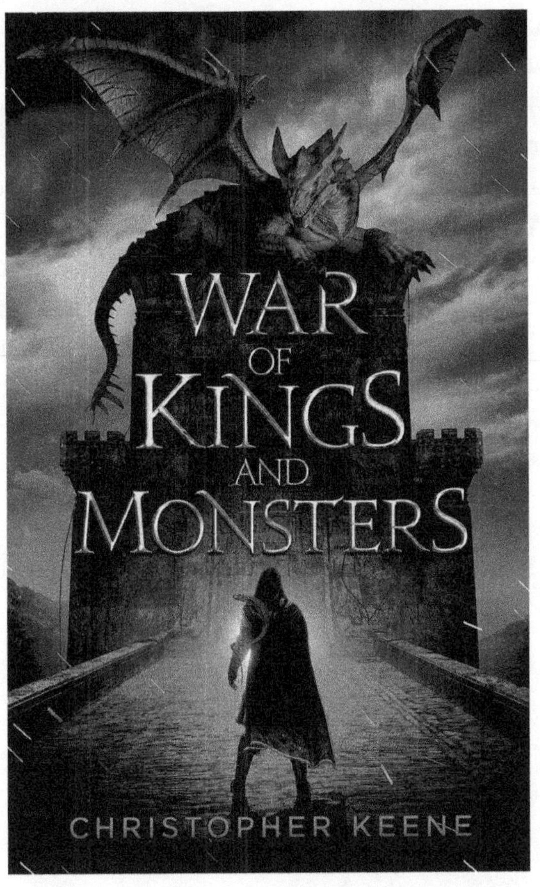

https://www.futurehousepublishing.com/books/war-of-kings-and-monsters/

Acknowledgments

Aidan Smith, to whom this book is dedicated, helped with developing some of the early ideas but credit should also go to those who were forced to read it in its infancy, generally in this order: Hayley Woolf, Zach Bethell, Jack Gifford, (this is generally where Aidan comes in also) and everyone else who gave the first chapters a look through. Heather Rubert really helped me to bring together the ending and interlinking plot, and credit should also go to Mandi Diaz, Alexa McKaig, Kennadie Halliday, Dara Johnson, Emma Heggem, and everyone else at Future House Publishing that worked on this with me. Thank you all.

Never miss a Future House release!

Sign up for the Future House Publishing email list:
www.futurehousepublishing.com/send-free-book

Connect with Future House Publishing

www.facebook.com/FutureHousePublishing

www.twitter.com/FutureHousePub

www.youtube.com/FutureHousePublishing

www.instagram.com/FutureHousePublishing

ABOUT THE AUTHOR

While studying for his Bachelor of Arts in English Literature from the University of Canterbury, New Zealand native Christopher Keene took the school's creative writing course in the hopes of someday seeing his own books on the shelves of his favorite bookstores. He is now the published author of *The Dream State Saga*, as well as his new epic fantasy *War of Kings and Monsters* and the *Super Dungeon* novelization *The Midnight Queen.* In his spare time, he writes a blog to share his love of the fantasy and science fiction genres in novels, films, comics, games, and anime (fantasyandanime.wordpress.com).

CPSIA information can be obtained
at www.ICGtesting.com
Printed in the USA
FSHW011204040521
81091FS

9 781950 020522